W9-BMH-628

M M

The Minor Third

The MAGIC MISFITS

The Minor Third

By Neil Patrick Harris
& Alec Azam

STORY ARTISTRY BY LISSY MARLIN

HOW-TO MAGIC ART BY KYLE HILTON

Little, Brown and Company

New York Boston

This book is a work of fiction. Names, characters, places, and incidents are the product of the author's imagination or are used fictitiously. Any resemblance to actual events, locales, or persons, living or dead, is coincidental.

Text and illustrations copyright © 2019 by Neil Patrick Harris.

Story illustrations by Lissy Marlin. How-To illustrations by Kyle Hilton.

Cover art by Lissy Marlin. Cover design by Karina Granda. Cover art copyright © 2019 by Neil Patrick Harris. Cover copyright © 2019 by Hachette Book Group, Inc.

Hachette Book Group supports the right to free expression and the value of copyright. The purpose of copyright is to encourage writers and artists to produce the creative works that enrich our culture.

The scanning, uploading, and distribution of this book without permission is a theft of the author's intellectual property. If you would like permission to use material from the book (other than for review purposes), please contact permissions@hbgusa.com. Thank you for your support of the author's rights.

Little, Brown and Company
Hachette Book Group
1290 Avenue of the Americas, New York, NY 10104
Visit us at LBYR.com

First Edition: September 2019

Little, Brown and Company is a division of Hachette Book Group, Inc. The Little, Brown name and logo are trademarks of Hachette Book Group, Inc.

The publisher is not responsible for websites (or their content) that are not owned by the publisher.

Library of Congress Cataloging-in-Publication Data
Names: Harris, Neil Patrick, 1973– author. | Azam, Alec, author. | Marlin, Lissy, illustrator. | Hilton, Kyle, illustrator.
Title: The magic misfits : the minor third / by Neil Patrick Harris & Alec Azam ; story artistry by Lissy Marlin ; how-to magic art by Kyle Hilton.
Description: First edition. | New York ; Boston : Little, Brown and Company, 2019. | Series: Magic Misfits ; 3 | Summary: New member Emily helps the Magic Misfits when a ventriloquist with a dastardly plan comes to town.
Identifiers: LCCN 2019005697| ISBN 9780316391870 (hardcover) | ISBN 9780316391900 (ebook) | ISBN 9780316391917 (library edition ebook)
Subjects: | CYAC: Magic tricks—Fiction. | Orphans—Fiction. | Ventriloquism—Fiction. | Friendship—Fiction. | Gay fathers—Fiction. | Humorous stories.
Classification: LCC PZ7.1.H3747 Maq 2019 | DDC [Fic]—dc23
LC record available at https://lccn.loc.gov/2019005697

ISBNs: 978-0-316-39187-0 (hardcover), 978-0-316-39190-0 (ebook), 978-0-316-42589-6 (large print), 978-0-316-42624-4 (int'l)

Printed in the United States of America

LSC-C

10 9 8 7 6 5 4 3 2 1

To my miraculous parents, Ron and Sheila,
for encouraging me to read and rite

TABLE OF CONTENTS

THE RETURN TO MINERAL WELLS

Psst!

Over here!

No, not behind that piece of furniture.

Over *here*!

No! Not in the other room.

The *other* over here...

Look closer. Closer. *Closer still...*

Yes! Here I am.

It's me...right in the pages of this book!

This ink is my voice, and these letters are messages from my mind.

How *mystical*, I know.

And there you are! How happy it makes me to have you along for yet another journey.

You will join me, will you not?

Apologies for the secrecy. But once you begin reading this—the third tale of the Magic Misfits—you shall understand why I was hiding. You see, the escapades in this book are a tad more treacherous than in the previous, and I want *you* to take as much care as the Misfits must themselves. I will need you to think twice about whom to trust and whom to blame. And if you examine every page, you might even find clues that answer questions you have not yet asked.

How *mysterious*, I know!

I have to assume that you remember the details of our favorite young magicians' club—the titular Magic Misfits. There is Carter (*The Vanisher*) Locke...Leila (*The Escape Artist*) Vernon...Theo (*The Levitator*) Stein-Meyer...and Ridley (*The Transformationist*) Larsen...and who could forget Olly and Izzy, the (*Hilarious*) Golden twins.

In the previous two books, our Misfits brought down a criminal circus enterprise run by the ominous B. B. Bosso and thwarted Sandra Santos (Madame

Esmeralda) and her crooked crew's attempt to acquire a secret ledger belonging to Dante Vernon—the owner of the local magic shop and one of Leila's dads (but of course you knew that). The Magic Misfits also rescued a monkey and a pair of field mice, and performed (twice!) at the majestic auditorium in the Grand Oak Resort, which overlooks their cozy town of Mineral Wells.

This seems like a lot of backstory, right? That's because it is! But don't worry if you can't remember. This adventurous third tale should fill in any gaps in your memory.

How *marvelous*, I KNOW!

With a lengthy setup like that, you must be itching to start the first chapter. But before that happens, I must insist we pause yet again to explain....

HOW TO...
Read This Book!

You probably know what is coming now: a lengthy explanation about how parts of this book contain the tales of the Magic Misfits, and how other parts of this book contain short magic lessons. You probably also remember that you are welcome to skip over those lessons and simply read the story parts. You are also welcome to stick this book in the sink, turn on the cold-water faucet, and let the pages soak for seven hours. But let's be honest: There are often things in life that we are *welcome to do* that we should *never, ever do.*

You probably *also* know (because you're quite sharp, aren't you?) that if you want to learn the skills presented in these magical lessons, you'll have to *practice, practice, practice.* And then take a nap, go to school, eat dinner, and then practice some more.

Over and over and over again. Because in order to make your friends believe your tricks, you are going to have to be fairly flawless.

So! Since you already know all these things—and if you didn't, now you do—I think that maybe it would be best for you to simply skip reading the rest of this section and move on. I wish I had suggested that earlier….

Oh, you're still here? How considerate! How diligent! Well then, the time is upon us. Go ahead. Take a deep breath. Focus. And turn the page….

ONE

Theo Stein-Meyer often dreamed about flying.

The dreams would begin with him lying in his bed, his parents snoring just down the hall. Then, as if by magic, he would find himself levitating several inches over his mattress. He would float over to his window, yank up the sash, then pull himself headfirst out into the night. Flying and swooping and swirling in the sky came to him as naturally as it did to his pet doves in the pen behind his house. He would simply squeeze something deep inside his mind, and his body would go.

Up! Up! Up! And farther still, up!

Directing himself through the sky, Theo felt just like he did while playing his violin—making melodies that skipped and flurried and sliced the air. Flying also reminded him of using his magic bow to make objects rise and dance in front of amazed audiences. You see, music and magic were Theo's two great loves. And he loved life best when he could do both at the same time.

On recent nights, however, his night-flying dreams had turned sinister. A shadowy figure moved through the town below Theo, a tall man in a top hat and cape, whose face was hidden in darkness. He was creeping through alleys and peering into houses. From way up high, Theo could hear him whispering secret enchantments that would make people do bad things.

The man's name was Kalagan, and he was responsible for much of the trouble Theo and his friends had faced together. The real Kalagan was a mesmerist who had lived in Mineral Wells long ago, but his henchmen had appeared in town several times over the summer, attempting to carry out his nefarious agenda, only to be thwarted by the Magic Misfits. Theo feared that Kalagan would soon return to Mineral Wells to deal with the Misfits himself.

In the dream, Theo swooped lower in the sky to eavesdrop on Kalagan, who had moved into the darkness of an alley. The shadows between buildings seemed to grow darker, more dangerous, and the man's whispering grew louder.

"Must…stop…Magic…Misfits…"

Kalagan was talking about Theo and his friends!

The mesmerist suddenly whipped around and reached up a hand toward the flying Theo, who shrieked as Kalagan dragged him down toward the ground.

"Must! Stop! Magic! Misfits!" the villain shouted.

Theo woke with a start, tangled in his sheets and gasping for breath. He struggled to free himself, taking deep breaths to calm down. He moved shakily to his window, where light at the line of trees near the horizon was bringing the late-summer morning to life. Was Kalagan somewhere nearby, looking back at him? Everything was quiet, but Theo knew the stillness would last only so long. (This is how the world works, after all.) But for now, he allowed it to seep into his skin and ease him back to sleep.

✳ ✳ ✳

Later that day, Mineral Wells was wide-awake and buzzing. Cars circled the center of town, passing quaint shops and stands while drivers looked for a rare parking space. Families strolled down sidewalks, while men in suits and women in smart dresses darted in and out of the town hall and the courthouse.

The air was warm and slightly humid, but an occasional breeze kept everyone comfortable. If the residents and visitors listened closely, they could hear a melody carried by that breeze—a lively waltz played on a violin. The musician was a boy dressed in a tuxedo, who had gathered with his friends at the gazebo in the town green to practice for the upcoming Mineral Wells talent show.

Theo danced his bow across the strings. His friends Carter, Leila, Ridley, Olly, and Izzy were standing to the sides. At Theo's feet, a teddy bear hopped and hovered as if it had been enchanted to life. When Theo sped up the waltz, the bear bounced more quickly, and when Theo slowed, the bear followed dreamily, as if listening.

As the song neared its climax, the bear began to rise up in front of Theo. One foot, two feet, three, four! And as Theo played the final note, he whipped his

violin and bow to the side as he reached out to catch the bear with his other hand. At the last moment, however, Theo's eyes caught on a darkly dressed figure in the distance, and his fist closed on empty air. It looked just like the evil man from his dreams.

"Theo!"

"Theo?"

"Hey, Theo!"

Theo blinked and looked around to find his friends staring at him. He shivered, unsure if his eyes had been playing tricks on him.

"What happened?" Ridley asked, her red curls vibrating as she shook her head. "That was so good up until the end!"

"I apologize," Theo answered, his cheeks flushing. "My mind wandered."

"All our minds have been doing that lately," Leila said, walking over to squeeze Theo's elbow in support.

"*My* mind hasn't only been wandering," said Olly. "It's been positively exploring!"

"Hiking!" proclaimed his twin sister, Izzy.

"Spelunking!"

"My mind took a steamer ship to Antarctica," Izzy said with a grin.

"*My* mind became friends with polar bears!" Olly countered.

"Wrong continent," Ridley said, cutting the twins off. She pressed a button on her wheelchair and a "wrong answer!" buzzer vibrated the gazebo. Then she smiled.

"The Magic Misfits have been through a lot," said Carter. "It's okay to have trouble concentrating sometimes, Theo."

Ridley sighed. "Not concentrating isn't going to help us win the talent show. We've got to stay focused. That prize money is nothing to scoff at."

The Mineral Wells Talent Show was less than two weeks away, and many residents of the town had already signed up to show off operatic voices, hula dances, tightrope walks, gymnastic routines, monologue recitations, and more.

"Who's scoffing?" said Carter. "It's more money than I've ever seen. If we win, I'll finally be able to pay everyone back for all their help since I came to Mineral Wells. And if there's any money left over, I'm getting one of those fancy cabinets that famous magicians use to make people disappear on stage!"

"You don't owe anybody anything," Leila argued back at her cousin. "Except maybe a smile now and then. If we win, I'm getting a Leila-sized water tank so I can practice holding my breath while breaking out of my straitjacket."

"Me and Olly are gonna get a couple pairs of the shiniest golden tap shoes the world's ever seen," Izzy jumped in.

"Speak for yourself, sis," Olly replied. "I'd rather buy myself some lessons in stage combat so I'll be ready for the next time we have to fight Kalagan's goons."

"Why not just take *real* combat lessons?" asked Ridley, rolling her eyes. "Then you'll be ready for fights that happen off stage too."

Olly's eyes lit up. "That's a great idea!"

Ridley gave him a small nod. "With that prize money, I'd upgrade my wheelchair with the new gadgets I've been working on. I could even make it transform.

A race car. An airplane. A tank! No one would mess with us then." She glanced at Theo, who was staring off into the distance again. "What about you, Theo? What would you use the prize money for?"

Theo came back to the group. "Skydiving lessons," he said simply. He took one more look around for the dark figure he thought he had seen, then went down the steps to retrieve the teddy bear. "Now, where were we?"

"You wanna try that ending again?" Ridley asked. "You *almost* had it."

The word buzzed in his head. It *almost* felt like an insult. But he had been friends with Ridley for as long as he could remember, and he knew she did not mean anything by it. "I have performed the trick fine before," said Theo. "I was simply distracted just now. Someone else can go."

Ridley came forward and made a great show of pulling a bunch of bananas from the pouch at the back of her chair. She asked a volunteer from the crowd (Leila) to pick one and peel it. But when Leila pulled at the banana's skin, the fruit inside fell to the ground in many distinct slices.

Carter went next and covered himself head to toe

with a large silk cape. He asked the twins to pull it away. When they did, Carter's head appeared to be missing! He stumbled around the gazebo until he bumped into Izzy, who was still holding the cape. Then he draped it back over himself. Seconds later, when he whipped the cape away, his head had reappeared.

"That was amazing!" Ridley exclaimed.

"Thanks!" said Carter. "I've been working on it for a couple weeks."

"Should we practice the finale?" Leila asked.

"We should definitely practice your routine," Ridley answered. "But are we sure we want to use it for the last act?"

"We can figure out who will go last later," said Leila. "For now..." She pointed to Theo, giving him his cue.

He raised his violin to his chin, and the jolt of a harsh chord echoed across the town green. Pedestrians stopped in their tracks on the sidewalk across the street.

"Move along!" Ridley called loudly. "Nothing to see here!"

Leila rolled her eyes at Ridley's typical gruffness and kept going. Her act was a re-creation of the break-in at Vernon's Magic Shop a couple of weeks ago, when

Kalagan's henchmen known as the "frown clowns" had attempted to steal Mr. Vernon's important notebook.

Theo was accompanying the trick with a moody melody on his violin as Leila quickly tied the clowns (played by Carter, Olly, Izzy, and Ridley) together with soft white rope. The makeshift villains formed a straight line across the gazebo, arms raised in front of themselves.

"Good people of Mineral Wells!" Leila called to a few passersby. "Our magic club needs a volunteer to check that these knots are solid. Is anyone willing to help?"

From around the town green, people stared, unsure if they should approach. Then a familiar group of five boys crossed the street.

Theo's bow slipped. A shriek echoed from his strings.

"We'll help you," said the largest of the five, coming to the bottom of the gazebo steps. The others flanked him. Up close, Theo was certain that these were the bullies who had bothered him and the other Misfits earlier in the summer. A squishy feeling settled in his stomach, and he felt a rustling of feathers at his ribs.

Carter, Olly, Izzy, and Ridley were all connected by

Leila's single white rope, and they looked as worried as Theo felt. Then, to his surprise, Leila waved the largest boy onto the gazebo platform. "Step right up," she said. "What's your name?"

"You know it's Tyler," he answered. Theo remembered that Leila knew these boys well, as they were her classmates during the school year. Since Theo attended private school, he luckily ran into them less.

Leila whispered to the bully, "*No funny business, Tyler.*"

Tyler whispered back, "But I'm hilarious." Then he smiled wide, showing his teeth.

"Hilarious-*looking*," Ridley murmured, and Tyler frowned at her. Theo wanted to step between them and demand that the boy get off the stage, but his tongue appeared to be stuck to the roof of his mouth.

Leila's voice came out like a squeak. "Please check the knots, *Tyler*, and make sure I tied up my friends tightly."

"Glad to," he said with a smirk, then pulled hard at the rope around Carter's wrists, pinching his pink skin.

"Ouch!" Carter cried.

"Hey!" Ridley yelled. "Knock it off!"

Tyler moved on to Olly and Izzy, pulling the knots tighter around their ankles.

The twins yelped.

"Quit it!" Leila scolded, pushing the boy's hands away from her friends. Tyler shoved her back. Theo felt chills of rage. He started to rush over, intending to thwack the jerk across the skull with his bow, when another idea popped into his head....

"You all think you're so amazing!" Tyler scoffed. "You're no better than the rest of us." His cronies sneered in agreement.

"We never said we were," said Leila. "We only want to make people smile."

"Mission accomplished," said Tyler. "I'm smiling."

Leila's own fake grin was gone. "Not for long," she muttered. She nodded at the tied-up Misfits, then clapped her hands over her head. Carter, Olly, Izzy, and Ridley made a swift movement.

And the rope disappeared! Standing on the stage, they were all free as birds.

And speaking of birds...

Theo opened his tuxedo jacket, releasing several white doves that he had been concealing for the grand finale. The doves circled the ceiling of the gazebo. When Theo clucked his tongue, the birds dive-bombed

Tyler, who stumbled, trying to escape their sharp beaks and claws. He teetered at the top step and then tumbled down into his friends at the bottom, sending them sprawling onto the grass.

"You were right!" Olly called out to the boy. "You *are* hilarious!"

"A genuine chuckle-factory!" added Izzy.

As the doves flew out from inside the gazebo to circle the town green, Tyler stood up and pointed at Theo. "You're gonna regret that!"

Straightening his tuxedo, Theo stuck out his tongue and released a long, musical raspberry. He waved his bow, as if conducting a symphony of spittle. The sound was so surprising that the bullies froze and stared at him.

You see, my friend, the raspberry was a misdirection, a classic magician's trick. It made the boys pause just long enough for the doves to receive Theo's signal—his bow waving in the air—and react.

Little white splashes rained down onto the heads of the bullies. *Splat! Splat! Splat!*

"Ugh," cried one of them, glancing upward, only to be greeted with a splash right on the tip of his nose.

"What *is* this?" asked another, wiping the goo from his hair.

"Those birds!" shrieked a third. "They're...*going to the bathroom* on us!"

"Gross!" shouted Tyler. "Run!"

The bullies scattered in all directions. Moments later, the doves settled onto the roof of the gazebo, awaiting further instruction.

"Is everyone all right?" Theo asked his friends.

"My wrists are a little sore," said Carter. "But at least the rope trick worked."

"You guys did great!" Leila chirped, retrieving the rope, which had recoiled by spring into a space inside Ridley's wheelchair. "Grace under pressure."

"Pressure?" echoed Carter.  "That felt more like torture."

"It was worth it," Izzy and Olly said in unison.

Theo waited for someone to mention his doves, but his hopes were interrupted by the unmis- takable sound of someone clapping.

The Misfits looked around. Theo worried that the bullies had come back. Instead, he saw a girl with long blond hair dressed all in black, including a beret that was tilted to the side of her head. She clapped slowly, like a ticking clock. With every smack of her hands, her feet stepped in time, bringing her closer and closer to the gazebo.

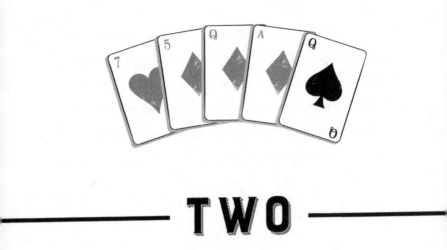

TWO

The girl in black had hypnotized the Misfits.

Theo stared as she crossed the lawn, unsure if she would become even more trouble than the group of boys. "Please tell me you all planned every moment of that," the girl said. "Bird poo included."

"We wish!" said Carter. "Might be something to remember for next time, though."

"I'll be sure to pick nicer volunteers during our actual performance," Leila added with a grimace.

Ridley cleared her throat. "And who are you?" she asked the girl.

"Oh, sorry. I'm Emily Meridian." *Meridian?* thought Theo. *Where have I heard that name before?* "I stay with my dad during the summer sometimes. The rest of the year, I'm with my mother in another town upstate."

Leila came down the steps and pulled Emily into a friendly hug. "Welcome to Mineral Wells! I'm Leila Vernon."

Emily squirmed at the unexpected embrace, but released a surprised giggle when Leila let go.

Ridley wheeled down the ramp straddling the gazebo staircase. "I'm Ridley Larsen. The boy with the violin is Theo Stein-Meyer. Carter Locke is the blue-eyed blond. And the twins are Olly and Izzy Golden. With Leila, we are the Magic Misfits."

"I know who you are," said Emily. "The whole town knows about you. And after seeing what you just did to those creeps, I'd say you're the ones to beat at the talent show."

Theo felt a flush of pride. "Are you participating too?" he asked.

Emily shook her head. "I don't really have a tal—"

Just then, from the bushes at the base of the gazebo, Tyler leapt up, clutching a handful of wet earth. He ratcheted his arm back before flinging the crud at Theo. It hit him, *WHUMP*, right in the chest, splattering across his white tuxedo shirt.

Before Theo could react, Emily bolted to the bully's side. "Leave them alone!"

"Or what?" Tyler moved to push her, but she swiveled, and he tripped past her. He reached out to grab her arm, but she swung it around, and Tyler ended up on the ground. "Ow!" he said through a mouthful of grass before turning onto his back.

"That was nothing, Tyler," Emily growled. Before he could get up, she placed her foot lightly on his chest, leaving a mark similar to the one the dirt had left on Theo. "If you don't want your mom to know how you've been treating my new friends, you'll knock it off. She's at my father's store right now. Should we walk back there together?"

"Get off me!" Tyler yelled as Emily put more weight on his chest.

"Promise you'll leave them alone," she warned.

"Fine! I won't do it again!"

Emily removed her foot and helped him up. Tyler gave her one last nasty look, then took off in search of his pals.

Theo was floored. He had seen plenty of magic before, especially after spending so much time with the Misfits at Mr. Vernon's magic shop. But he had not experienced anything so spectacular as this girl taking out an oaf six inches taller than her and at least twenty pounds heavier.

"That was—" Carter started.

"—*awesome!*" Leila finished.

"Impressive," Ridley decided.

Olly and Izzy immediately began to re-create the scuffle on the gazebo platform, adding gymnastic flourishes and staccato tap-dance moves.

"Thank you, Emily," Theo added. He placed his

violin gently on the floor so he could wipe the clump of mud from his stomach. "But were you not worried about him hurting you?"

"That doofus?" Emily smirked. "No way. I've known Tyler since he was still eating mashed peas. Even better, our parents are close friends. He knows I'll tell his mother if he's bothering someone. It takes a lot worse to scare me."

"Us too," said Carter, clutching his suspenders. Then he glanced around nervously. "Usually."

"You said your father owns a store," Theo mentioned. "Which one?"

"Meridian's Music," Emily answered. "It's just down the street."

"Of course! I go there all the time with my father. Meridian's is where he bought me this very violin. Does this mean your father is—"

"Mick Meridian. The owner. He's the best at what he does."

"I couldn't agree more." Theo raised his hand, and his violin lifted up off the floor. When its neck met his palm, he brought his bow to the strings and played a quick, happy melody.

His friends all clapped, while Emily nodded. "Pretty."

"I did not know Mr. Meridian had a daughter," said Theo.

Emily frowned. "You mean...he's never mentioned me?"

Theo blushed. "I am sure he would have—"

Emily grinned. "I'm kidding!" She knocked his shoulder lightly. "My dad's pretty busy while he's at the store. It's not a big deal."

Theo chuckled self-consciously. He suddenly felt a little too warm.

Across the street, a bell jingled as the door to Vernon's Magic Shop swung open. "Leila! Carter!" called Mr. Vernon, standing in the entry. "Change-O has been racing around the store nonstop. As wonderful as I think it is that you've been practicing with your friends, I would appreciate it if you would come feed him before he knocks over another jar of fake eyeballs!" Mr. Vernon's curly white hair sprang from his head like a shock of whipped potatoes, and his black mustache sat on his upper lip like a smear of tapenade. He wore his usual dark, formal suit, shiny black shoes, a top hat, and a long cape tied at his neck. The first time Theo had encountered Mr. Vernon, he had been so taken with the tuxedo the magician had been wearing that Theo had become inspired to wear them too.

A hunger pang gurgled in Theo's belly, and he realized how late the day had grown. He pulled a chain watch from his jacket pocket. "Oh good," he said. "I still have time before dinner. My parents hate it when I am late."

"Do they hate you being late?" asked Ridley. "Or do they just wish you spent more time practicing your violin?"

"A little of both."

"But they'd have to be impressed by that bird poo trick!" Emily said with a laugh.

"I doubt they would want to know about it," Theo replied sheepishly.

"Coming, Dad!" Leila answered. She glanced at her friends. "You guys want to help feed the monkey?"

"Not if he feeds me first!" Izzy joked.

Ridley shook her head. "That...doesn't make sense."

"What if he *eats* you first?" asked Olly.

"Change-O wouldn't hurt a fly," Carter said.

"Too bad, because I hear they're highly nutritious," Izzy said with a wink.

"Let's go," Ridley said. "Mr. Vernon is getting sick of holding the door open." She was right—Mr. Vernon was tapping his foot, and with each tap, a red handkerchief bounced up and down in the pocket of his black jacket—a flashing alarm.

The group looked both ways at the edge of the road. Ridley peered at Emily. "Oh, *you're* coming too?"

Emily nodded. "Wouldn't miss it. I've always wanted to meet a monkey. You don't mind, do you, Leila?"

"He's *Carter's* monkey," Ridley corrected.

"It's okay," Carter answered, with a hint of skepticism.

Ridley pursed her lips and moved her chair forward, managing to hold her sharp tongue.

As they reached the magic shop's door, Theo's doves cooed from the roof of the gazebo, where they pecked at the weathered green shingles. Theo wasn't worried, though. He knew the birds would follow him home when he was ready. For now, he wished only to learn more about the mysterious new girl who was walking beside him.

HOW TO...

Find a Spectator's Card

I bet you would like to know more about the mysterious girl dressed in black too. But wait...we have a new trick to learn first!

You will want to practice this one very hard, because it will come in handy when combined with another trick I will share later. Maybe place a bookmark near this page so you can easily find it again. (If you do not have a bookmark, a feather will work. Or a rose petal. Or a fake mustache! You keep those in your bedroom, right? I do as well.)

WHAT YOU'LL NEED:

A regular deck of playing cards

STEPS:

1. Before you start, memorize the card on the bottom of the deck. We will call this card the *key card*.

KEY CARD!

2. Spread the cards out, facedown. Ask a volunteer to pick one of the cards. Tell them to show the card to the rest of the audience, but make sure you turn away so you do not see it.

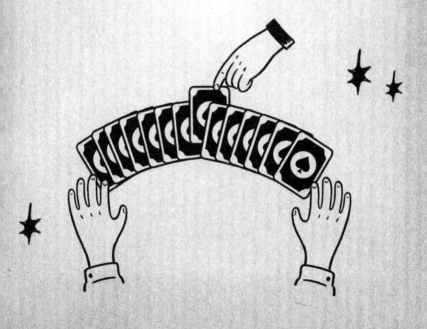

3. Separate the deck into two piles, and then ask your volunteer to place their card on top of the first pile. Take the second pile and place it on top of the volunteer's card, bringing the full deck back together. The card that you have memorized (the key card) should now be directly on top of the volunteer's card. *(Reminder: You still do not know which card the volunteer has chosen.)*

4. Hand the deck to the volunteer and ask them to cut the deck several times. *(Cutting a deck means separating the deck into two piles, then taking the bottom pile and placing it on top of the other pile.)* When your volunteer is ready, take back the deck.

5. Spread the cards out, this time faceup, so that you can see them.

6. Locate the card you memorized— the *key card!* The key card will be directly *underneath* the card that the volunteer chose.

THEIR CARD! →   ⟵ KEY CARD!

Hint: If you find the *key card* on the top of the deck, the volunteer's card will be the card on the bottom of the deck.

7. Present them with their card! Be as creative as you like about what you say when presenting.

8. Now take a bow!

THREE

It always amazed Theo how magical Vernon's Magic Shop felt, even as he entered for what might have been the thousandth time. The air seemed to shimmer. Light from the front window reached the farthest parts of the farthest wall, illuminating dusty volumes of cracked leather books marked with mysterious symbols. There were tables crammed with crystal balls, playing cards, and packets of flash paper. Racks of robes, capes, multicolored scarves, and satin black top hats crowded another area. (Also, a rabbit *named* Top Hat was hopping up and down the aisles! *Silly*, I know!)

"I've barricaded Change-O," said Mr. Vernon, nodding slightly to the rear bookcases. "In the *you-know-what*."

The Misfits moved toward the hidden space behind the shelves, the room their magic club used for meetings. But Ridley glided ahead of everyone, then spun around, clearing her throat loudly. "Here is far enough," she said, raising an eyebrow at Emily.

A telltale screeching immediately sounded from behind the bookcases.

Emily looked as if she were trying to suppress a smile. "Let me guess. There's a concealed door in these shelves. And behind it is the monkey."

"Why would you think that?" Carter asked guiltily.

"Don't tell us you're a psychic," said Olly. "We just had a really bad experience with one of those."

"I'll test her," said Izzy, skipping forward. She stared into Emily's eyes. "What shape am I thinking of? If you say triangle, I'll be amazed. Oh, wait..."

"I'm not psychic," Emily answered. "It's just...I can clearly hear a monkey screeching behind that wall."

Suddenly, Mr. Vernon was standing beside the group. "Very astute, young lady," he said, holding out a white-gloved hand to Emily. When she went to shake it, a shimmery bouquet of silver flowers appeared, and he gave them to her instead. Her eyes grew wide with surprise.

"This is Emily," Theo said. "Her father owns the music shop down the street, where I got my violin. She's visiting for the summer."

Mr. Vernon tilted his head, a look of recognition glinting in his gaze. "Of course! How is my old friend Mick?"

"Dad's doing pretty well. Thanks." Emily shook his hand. "Nice to see you again, Mr. Vernon."

"Funny that it doesn't happen more often, Emily. Most young people who live in Mineral Wells tend to set foot inside my magic shop at least *once* a year."

"But I don't live in Mineral Wells," Emily answered. "And besides, I'm not so much into magic."

The shimmery feeling of the shop suddenly disappeared. Theo felt his stomach go cold, but then he remembered that the mud was still drying there.

When Emily noticed everyone's expressions, she stammered, "I—I *like* magic. I'm just not any good at it. Not like you guys. Mr. Vernon, have you seen what they can—"

"I've seen," Mr. Vernon interrupted with a smile.

The atmosphere in the shop returned to normal. He raised an eyebrow at the group. "How was the latest rehearsal? Tricky, no?"

"We were doing fine until Theo dropped the teddy bear," Ridley stated.

Theo felt his skin tingle with embarrassment. "I think Mr. Vernon was talking about when those boys were bothering us." He pointed at the stain on his shirt.

"I was," Mr. Vernon answered. "Are you all right, my friend?"

"He's fine," said Olly.

"It's just that his mind has been wandering," said Izzy.

"My mind is fine," Theo said, trying not to sound frustrated.

Mr. Vernon crouched to meet Theo's eyes. "Are you certain? Is something worrying you?"

He did not wish to talk about it with Emily there, but Theo finally let his shoulders sink. "I thought I saw Kalagan today. That was why I messed up my act. A man dressed all in black with a cape and top hat was standing in the town green. Watching us."

The Misfits glanced at one another nervously.

"*Kalagan?*" Mr. Vernon asked. "That seems highly unlikely. You might consider another possibility...." He gestured to himself, dressed in black, with a cape and top hat gracing his shoulders and head.

"Wait..." Theo scrunched up his forehead. "It was you?"

Mr. Vernon's eyes twinkled. "Let's just say I wanted to get a closer look at your progress."

"So Kalagan wasn't spying on us?" Carter asked.

Screeeeeeech!

Everyone jumped as the monkey again demanded attention. Ridley moved toward the bookshelves. "Emily, close your eyes for a second!" She grabbed the volume that triggered the door, and suddenly, Change-O was racing around the shop. Ridley put the book back and the door slid shut.

With her eyes still closed, Emily asked, "Who is Kalagan?"

"A bad man who has been trying to do bad things in Mineral Wells," said Theo. "His story is long and sordid."

Emily opened her eyes. "You'll have to tell me more sometime." Change-O leapt onto the counter beside her, and Emily shrieked, then laughed.

"Mr. Vernon," said Carter, "would you hand me Change-O's food sack?"

"I'm afraid I cannot," answered Mr. Vernon.

"*Da-aad,*" said Leila. "Don't be silly. The bag is right behind the counter."

"Who's being silly? Certainly not me. Certainly not when the food sack is right where it should be. Don't trip!"

Carter wobbled as his heels banged into the food sack, which had suddenly appeared on the floor behind him. He chuckled. "Thanks, Mr. Vernon." He untied the bag and poured some of the grains and nuts into Change-O's bowl. The monkey dashed forward and began greedily stuffing his mouth. From the balcony overhead, Leila's yellow-naped Amazon parrot let out a jealous screech.

Leila held out her hand. "Presto, come!" The bird flew down and landed on her shoulder. Emily reached out carefully, and Presto nuzzled her knuckles.

"*Hula girl, spoil magic-skull! Battle lava vapor!*" said the bird.

Emily looked impressed and confused at the same time, but the Misfits were so used to the parrot's occasional strange ramblings that none of them even blinked. "How did you move that food sack without us noticing, Mr. Vernon?" she asked.

"By staying one step ahead of the game," Vernon proclaimed, his hand on his chest. "Something I would recommend to you talent show contestants." He went on, "Aspiring magicians should be ready for anything. And they must prepare several *outs* in case of the unexpected."

"What's an *out*?" asked Izzy.

"The opposite of an *in*, of course," said Olly, poking her shoulder.

Carter shook his head. "It's that a magician should always have a plan in case things go screwy. Right, Mr. Vernon? Me and my uncle Sly learned every exit whenever we went into a new boarding home...I mean, *house*." Carter was still getting used to living with the Vernons. His scam-artist uncle had moved them around so much that Carter still slept on his bedroom floor sometimes, worried that he might need to wake quickly. At least, that was what Carter had told Theo the last time he decided to open up about his past.

"Exactly," said Mr. Vernon. "Before you walk on

stage, you must practice and prepare for multiple outcomes. Expect the unexpected. In fact, this is helpful advice for living your lives as well. Start thinking this way, and I believe you'll find that a dead end can be *more* than just a dead end."

"You mean like an ending is sometimes another beginning?" asked Leila.

"Perceptive, Leila." Mr. Vernon smiled mysteriously. "A dead end can also be a rallying point, or a secret door, or a trap for your antagonists." He glanced around the group. "Not everyone can be as strong and agile as your new friend Emily here."

Emily shrugged, unembarrassed. "I've taken martial arts classes. I'm not that strong, but I do know how to push someone off balance."

"A worthy skill indeed. And it came in handy today while these magicians were backed up against a proverbial wall."

"Are you saying we need to learn karate, Dad?" Leila asked.

"Only if you want to, my dear. But what I'm saying is, magic can work wonders too."

"And music!" Theo added, thinking of the way

his violin could so easily distract and entrance specta-
tors.

"Speaking of which," said Emily, "I should probably head back to the shop. My dad tends to worry when
I disappear."

"Why would he worry?" Olly asked.

"Whenever someone disappears, we applaud!" Izzy
proclaimed with a flourish.

Emily laughed and waved good-bye, even to Presto
and Change-O, then slipped out the front door.

"It was nice of you to invite her over, Leila," said
Mr. Vernon. "Everyone needs a friend or two."

"I agree," said Leila, setting Presto on her perch
next to the register.

"Wait a second," said Ridley, holding up her hands.
"Who says that she's our friend?"

"She helped us," said Leila. "That's what friends do."

"But the Magic Misfits doesn't need more members."

"She never said she wanted to be a Misfit," Theo
said. "She didn't seem to want to do magic at all."

"I've learned that non-magical friends make the
best audience members," said Mr. Vernon, tilting his

hat and letting out a small windup dragonfly, which zipped around the store just over everyone's heads. "With friends, you can always be sure *someone* will show up!"

"Well, I like her," said Leila.

"Me too," said Olly.

"Me seven," said Izzy.

Theo wanted to say the same ("Me too," not "Me seven"), but for some reason, his tongue felt tied in

knots. After a moment, he untangled the insides of his mouth and said, "If we ask her to...tag along...maybe she could protect us from jerks like that Tyler guy."

"We can protect ourselves just fine," Ridley shot back.

"Yes, you are quite lucky to be part of a group that looks out for one another," Mr. Vernon said. He then went to answer the shop's ringing phone.

"Friendship doesn't need a reason," said Leila, reaching out and catching the mechanical dragonfly.

"It'll be nice to have a new person to play jokes on," said Olly.

"Whatever the reason," said Theo, "I think we should invite Emily to our next rehearsal. She was..." Words flickered through his head. He landed on a harmless one: "She was different."

"Different?" asked Ridley. "Different than what?"

Theo was careful about what he said next. "Than the usual. Nothing. Never mind."

Ridley rolled her eyes as she turned toward the secret door once again. Theo flinched. *Why would she do that?* He was used to Ridley's brusqueness, but she'd seemed particularly agitated all day.

At the front counter, Mr. Vernon's tone shifted,

grew intense. "Interesting," he said into the telephone receiver. He noticed the kids glance over at him and turned his back. Still, Theo could make out bits of the whispered conversation. "Obviously, we need to address this immediately....Yes, I can come.... Tonight..."

After he hung up, Mr. Vernon looked worried. It was something Theo had seen in the older magician's eyes only once before—during the battle in the magic shop weeks earlier, when the former frown clowns had attacked them.

Leila dashed to his side. "Dad, what's wrong?"

"It seems I have to leave town."

"What? Why?" Carter asked.

Mr. Vernon spoke carefully. "Remember the list of names from my ledger? The people in my magician society whom I was trying to protect?" The group nodded, almost as one. "Apparently some of them have been compromised. By Kalagan himself."

"I thought compromise was a good thing," said Carter.

Mr. Vernon shook his head. "Different kind of compromise, Carter. Kalagan's reach is wider than we previously thought, and he's managed to get information about our members that could be used against them. And he might have found another way to get to us. I need to meet with the members and plan a course of action."

"Let us come with you!" said Leila. "We can help."

"You'll be more help to me here in Mineral Wells, where you're safe," he answered. "Besides, someone needs to keep an eye on all these animals."

"Who are you calling an animal?" Izzy asked, raising her fists in a mock boxing stance.

"He means the *actual* animals," Olly said, raising his own fists. "Top Hat. Presto. Change-O. *And* our mice back at the resort."

"Oh, I see," said Izzy. "So why are we fighting again?"

"If you'll excuse me," said Mr. Vernon, heading to the staircase, "I have to check the train schedule and then pack, and I must call the Other Mr. Vernon and let him know what's going on."

"Can we at least go with you to the station?" asked Theo.

"I suppose that would be fine," said Mr. Vernon,

"if it's fine with all your parents. It's getting rather late."

Theo grimaced. He was sure his parents would *not* be fine with it.

But sometimes friends come first.

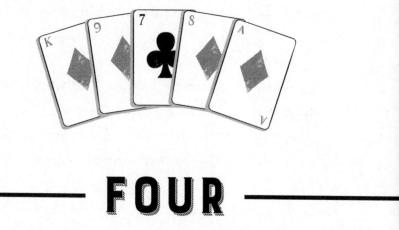

FOUR

Less than an hour later, the Misfits arrived with the two Mr. Vernons at the Mineral Wells train station. The Other Mr. Vernon had come home early from work in his wood-paneled station wagon. He drove Theo, Ridley, and Carter. Dante rode with Leila, Olly, and Izzy in a big yellow taxi. They all waited quietly as Mr. Vernon purchased his ticket, and then they followed him outside to the platform.

Theo glanced up and down the track in both directions. The lines of the rails stretched off into the distance. He could not picture where Mr. Vernon was headed, mostly because Mr. Vernon had refused to tell them exactly where he was going. He suspected only the Other Mr. Vernon knew for sure.

Theo had not called his parents. He glanced at the other Misfits, two in particular. Leila's big eyes were watery, and Carter looked as worried as Theo had ever seen him. As friends, they were worth getting in trouble for.

"Will you call when you get there?" Leila asked her dad.

"I'm not sure if I'll be able to," said Mr. Vernon. "But I'll try."

"Should we be worried about Kalagan coming here?" asked Carter.

The Other Mr. Vernon placed his hand on the boy's shoulder. "Not while I'm around." Carter squeezed the hand, but his face still looked troubled.

"But, Poppa, you have to work at the resort," Leila chided. "Isn't it the busy season?"

"Oh, it's always the busy season." He rubbed his trim beard. "My staff can pick up the slack. What's most important is you all. We can make it work."

"*I* think we can take care of ourselves," Ridley muttered. "We've done it before."

Mr. Vernon raised an eyebrow. "This is no time to develop a big head. Hubris is a vice."

"Who's Hugh Briss?" asked Izzy innocently. "And when is he turning thirteen?"

"I'm pretty sure he's a clothing designer," answered Olly.

"*Hubris*," Mr. Vernon repeated. "*Pride*. It makes a magician lazy. Remember what I said back at the shop: Expect the unexpected." He glanced at Ridley. "You never know when a spectator will try to trip you up." And at the twins. "Or when you might miscalculate your timing." To Carter. "Or when you'll draw the wrong card." To Leila. "Or when you'll tie the knots too tightly." And Theo. "Remember to make sure that several objects on stage are light enough to float and fly, for when something goes amiss. Then practice and prepare for multiple outcomes. Notice I said *when*, not *if*. One day, something will fall inevitably out of place. Do not be caught unaware. Think things through. And try to keep control away from those who would wrest it from you."

"We will, Dad," said Leila. "We promise."

"We promise," the others echoed together. Then they glanced at one another and smiled at the coincidence.

"And most important..." Mr. Vernon leaned down and lowered his voice. "Never lose sight of what bonds you. Your friendship, your loyalty, your love for each other."

"*Love?*" said Ridley. "Gross."

"It's not, really," Mr. Vernon answered with a soft smile. "I'm not talking about romance, Ridley. Love can also be about connection. You six will always be stronger together. Remember that."

A whistle sounded from far down the track. The train was approaching. The Other Mr. Vernon stepped between the group and the platform edge, motioning everyone backward to safety. Soon, the great black steam engine appeared, piping clouds of smoke up into the sky. It rumbled to a stop at the far end of the platform, a long line of passenger cars behind it. Out of nowhere, a crowd had formed, every person holding tickets and baggage and souvenirs from the Grand Oak Resort on the hill. A conductor bounced down a couple of steps from the closest car and called out, "*Alllll aboard!*"

"And now it's time for me to take my leave!" Mr. Vernon said dramatically. He kissed Leila's cheek and the crown of Carter's head and waved to everyone else. After embracing his husband, he flipped his cape off his shoulder and waved it in front of his bag. When he whipped the cape away, the bag had disappeared. The kids gasped, then cheered. The magician gave a gracious bow. He held the cape up before him. Seconds later, it dropped to the ground. But the man was nowhere to be seen, having vanished into the smoky air.

"Dad!" Leila cried out, worried.

In the window of the closest car, Mr. Vernon's top hat rose up. Below the hat was his smiling face. He

waved at the kids from behind the glass. The Other Mr. Vernon bent down and grabbed the rumpled cape from the platform. "Dante!" he called, holding it up. "Don't forget this!"

Mr. Vernon cracked the window open and reached out. The Other Mr. Vernon handed over the cape, holding on just a little longer than he needed to.

"See you all soon," Mr. Vernon said as the conductor climbed aboard, and the train pulled out of the station.

★ ★ ★

"You're late, Theo," said Leo.

"We had to set the table ourselves," said Gio.

"*I* set the table, Gio," said Cleo.

"And *I* am starving, Cleo," said Fiona. "Let's eat."

Theo's older siblings had arrived home several days earlier for their yearly summer visit. They were Leonard, Giovanni, Cleopatra, and Fiona, but everyone called them Leo, Gio, Cleo, and Fiona. Leo was the oldest. He played cello in an orchestra in New York City. Gio was next in line, and he was the bass guitarist in a popular wedding band outside San Francisco. Cleo was the middle sibling. She taught piano at a prestigious music school

in Boston. And Fiona, the youngest, sang mezzo-soprano in operas all around the world. Their talents were intimidating. Theo spent an excessive amount of time worrying that he would never live up to their already vast accomplishments.

From the dining room, they stared at him in the doorway. Ever since they had arrived, there had barely been enough room to walk down the hall without bumping elbows with one of them. "I am so sorry, everyone," he said, warmth filling his cheeks. "My friends and I had to deal with an emergency."

Mrs. Stein-Meyer's eyes went wide. "An emergency? Is everyone okay? Are you okay, Theo?" She rushed over to him and held her hand to his forehead.

"I am fine, Mother," he answered. "My friends and I were rehearsing for the town talent show. But then Mr. Vernon was called away at the last moment, and we had to see him off at the train station."

"What kind of emergency is that?" asked Leo. He shook his head.

"And what happened to your shirt?" asked Gio.

Theo glanced at the spot on his chest. It was still damp. He thought of the bullies in the park. "It got dirty, so I rinsed it off in the sink at the magic shop."

"Are you still playing around with that kid stuff, little brother?" chirped Fiona. "I thought by now you'd have grown out of *magic*."

Theo felt stung by his older sister's condescending tone. What he wanted to say was *I hope I will never grow out of magic*. But instead, he answered, "I have not."

Mr. Stein-Meyer sighed. "Go clean yourself up and take a seat. Your mother and I made our famous cherry-walnut meat loaf. And it is getting cold."

Theo ran up the stairs to his bedroom, put on a clean, crisp white shirt, added his bow tie and jacket, and then joined his family downstairs.

Finally, his mother smiled. "Oh, I am so happy we can all be together like this. I wish that each of you lived closer to home."

Theo found himself fighting with a nasty thought that was fluttering around inside his head: *I wish the exact opposite*.

✦ ✦ ✦

Later, after Theo had put on his pajamas and turned out his light, his mind began to wander. He thought of Emily Meridian and the move she'd done to take down that bully, Tyler. The swivel, the step, the twist.

She was so skilled! But it was the memory of her smile that made him feel funny in his chest.

The next thing Theo knew, he was flying high over Mineral Wells, and Emily was floating beside him. In the moonlight, her hair lifted from her head like seagrass swaying in an ocean current. The stars shone brightly, and the town below looked like the miniature play set in the front window of the toy store on Main Street. Theo was thankful that Kalagan was nowhere to be seen.

"Follow me," Emily whispered. And then they were swooping and diving, the night air whipping at their faces. They both yelled out, hollering as they dipped and rose up again, crisscrossing the night sky. Theo grinned, hoping his dream would not end too soon.

The sound of cooing doves filled his ears. He looked around, assuming his birds had joined his and Emily's wild flight. But then he realized that the noise was not coming from his mind. His eyes snapped open, and he sat up to find his doves nestled on his windowsill with only the screen separating them from his bedroom.

He had forgotten all about them!

Theo flung back his covers and shoved his feet into his slippers. Then he raced downstairs to the rear door, which led out to the backyard, where the bird coop sat, only partially filled.

The air was cool and a breeze sent goose bumps across his skin. He glanced up at his window and, finding the birds still sitting there, he clicked his tongue, instructing them to come down. He opened the door to the pen and the three doves joined the others, who tittered and fluttered, annoyed at being awakened.

Theo smacked his forehead. "Foolish, foolish, foolish," he whispered to himself. How could he have just left his pets out there in the town green? The birds could have been eaten by cats! Or coyotes! Or bears! (Well, maybe not bears. Bears eat bigger things, like siblings, teachers, and parents. Quick, *go warn them*! Back again so soon? Whew. That was close!)

Had Theo been too focused on Emily to remember the doves? Or had Mr. Vernon's leaving been the distraction? Maybe all the madness that had come through Mineral Wells just that summer was beginning to take a toll, Theo worried. He could never admit this mistake to the Misfits. After his mix-up during their rehearsal, they'd start to wonder if something was truly wrong. He wanted them to believe that he was as perfect as anyone they'd ever known. He was certain that was why they liked to keep him around—because he impressed them. With his tuxedos. With his diction. With the secret of his levitating violin bow.

But Theo had to admit: It was exhausting being so perfect all the time.

A deep resonance filled the air around him, vibrating his already prickled skin. He turned to find Leo, his oldest brother, sitting in the garden, his cello propped between his legs. Theo held his breath. Leo pulled his bow across the strings, allowing them to sing mysteriously. His skin appeared almost indigo in the moonlight. After a moment, Leo looked up, catching his brother's gaze.

"What are you doing out here, Leo?" Theo asked.

"I didn't get in enough practice today, and I can't play in the house right now. I'd wake up everyone."

"But the windows are open," said Theo. "They will still hear you."

"Then let my music be a lullaby." Leo smiled. "What are *you* doing out here, little brother?"

"I...was just checking on my birds. I wanted to make sure they were all here."

"But they weren't, were they?"

Leo must have seen Theo call the birds down from the window ledge. Theo lowered his gaze and shook his head.

"What's going on with you, Theo? You haven't been yourself since Gio, Cleo, Fiona, and I got here."

Theo wasn't sure what to say. Did he even know how to *be himself* around his family? "Some strange events from this summer have been clouding my mind," he finally said. "But it is nothing I cannot handle."

"I'm sure you're right," Leo answered. "But if not, you know what always helps bring my feet back to the ground?" Theo shook his head. "My music."

Theo held back a sigh. He knew where this conversation was going, and he did not want to follow.

"Father says that your practicing has been slipping. Is it true?"

"I have been practicing other things."

"Magic."

"Yes. Magic. My friends and I have gotten very good. Better than most in this little town."

"Impressive," Leo said. "But children can be very good at things that they will have no use for later in life." *Children?* Theo flinched at the word as if it were an insult. But his brother went on, "What do you plan on doing with…magic?"

Theo wanted to say, *Make people smile, spend time with my friends, protect this town from the evil forces threatening to overwhelm it*. He knew this last bit might sound a little dramatic.

"I'm not trying to tell you what to do." Leo stood and put his arm around Theo's shoulders. "But I know from experience that at your age, everything starts to change. And your musical talent is like the sea. Right now, the crest of a wave is rising. You either ride that wave into the future, or you miss it."

Theo was quiet for a beat. Then he said, "You sound like Father."

"Good," said Leo. "You should listen to us. We've had experiences that you have not." Theo stared into his brother's intense eyes and thought, *I could say the same*. "Father and Mother told us that you've gotten into some trouble this summer? The 'strange events' you mentioned?"

Dizziness crept into Theo's head. Leo was talking about Bosso and Sandra and Kalagan. "So *that* is what this is about," he said.

"Everyone just wants you to be safe," said Leo. Theo let out a long breath. "You're frustrated with me, I can tell. And that's fine. I'll say no more about it except this: Friends come and go, but we're your family, and we always will be. I've been watching you since you were born, and you have real talent, Theo. Talent that could last a lifetime...but *only* if you practice."

Theo nodded, feeling his frustration disperse into the cool darkness. Songs of crickets and tree frogs swelled from the nearby woods. He hugged Leo good night, went back inside, and crept into his bed.

As he closed his eyes, he listened to his brother's mournful melody playing in the garden just outside, and he considered what Leo had said about keeping his feet on the ground.

There would be no more dreams of flying, at least not that night.

FIVE

In the morning, Theo played the violin for his father, who gave him pointers and encouragement. Theo enjoyed their time together and could see that his father was pleased as well.

So when Ridley called and asked him to go with her up to the resort, Theo kept his expression neutral. He didn't need any more confrontation with his family. The phone was located in the crowded living room, and he did not want his siblings to know that he was speaking with one of his magical friends. "Izzy and Olly have something they want to show us," Ridley said. "They say it's important."

Theo dressed in a clean tuxedo and then told his mother where he was going. "Make sure you're home to set the table," she said quietly, so the others would not hear. "No excuses this time. And *no* emergencies."

"Yes, Mother," he said. And with that, he was out the door to meet Ridley, Carter, and Leila, heading for the road that would take them to the Golden twins.

The Grand Oak Resort was perched high on the hill overlooking the town of Mineral Wells. With its white clapboard siding, green shutters, and dark gabled roof, it had an air of country elegance, which made it stand out from the few other hotels in the county. People came from far and wide to participate in an array of activities at the resort: dancing, swimming, sailing, gymnastics, tree-climbing, and lounging in the mineral-rich waters of the natural spas that bubbled up from deep under the earth. The resort had stood since long before Theo was born, and he was certain it would still be standing by the time he was grown. There was the main building filled with guest rooms, a restaurant (run by the Other Mr. Vernon), a grand auditorium that held performances both large and small, and several outer buildings where the guests danced, lounged, took classes, and played games.

The Magic Misfits had recently learned that the resort was filled with decades-old secrets and mysteries, including the fact that Mr. Vernon's old magic club, the Emerald Ring, used to meet in the decrepit rear wing of the lodge, a portion of the main building that was now mostly abandoned. Earlier in the summer, some guests had been worried that the place was haunted, but after exposing Madame Esmeralda—Sandra Santos—as a fraud, the Misfits had been able to put that rumor, and several others, to rest.

However, one rumor that the Misfits had trouble removing from their minds was that a young Dante Vernon had been responsible for starting a fire that had ruined the rear wing in the first place. One of the bellhops had shared that information with the kids several weeks earlier, and it was a doozy. None of them could imagine that their kindly magician mentor would have done such a horrible thing. When they had asked him, Mr. Vernon had implied that Kalagan was the real perpetrator. But he was still less than forthcoming with answers.

Waiting by the elevator in the lobby with Ridley,

Carter, and Leila, Theo asked, "Does anyone know what the twins need to show us?"

Leila shook her head. "They were very mysterious about it on the telephone."

Ridley rolled her eyes. "I bet this is just the setup for one of their elaborate practical jokes."

"At least we get to see where they live," Theo said with a smile. The elevator dinged, and the doors parted. Theo followed everyone into the car.

This would be the first time he would meet the twins in their suite, and he didn't know what to expect. Plaid wallpaper? A recorded laugh track that played when you walked through the door? A metal floor that made tap-dancing sounds when you stepped on it?

"Did everyone have a good night?" Ridley asked as the doors shut with a *ding*.

"Absolutely perfect," said Theo with a thin-lipped grimace.

"That's so nice!" Leila answered, missing his expression. Her brow dropped as she added, "Our house felt strange without my dad there. He never did call to let us know that he arrived...wherever he was going."

"I'm *sure* he's fine," said Carter, his voice wobbling with the opposite of sureness.

"He's a smart cookie." Ridley nodded. "I trust he knows what he's doing. Who's watching the magic shop?"

Leila smoothed her hair. "Poppa decided that the shop should be closed while Dad is on his business trip. Hopefully it won't be for too long. Presto will miss talking to the customers."

"And Change-O will miss throwing things at them," sighed Carter. "I'm working on getting him to stop that."

The elevator doors opened and the group moved into an opulent hallway. The floors were dark wood, and long runners with intricate ochre and brown swirls covered most of them. Copper-and-glass sconces clung to the walls. Stripes of shadow appeared every few feet, providing enough mystery to keep everyone on their toes.

"This way," said Leila. "I think."

The group followed her until they reached a doorway marked 315. Vintage big-band music was blasting from within. Carter knocked and knocked but no one answered. "Are we sure this is their room?"

Ridley raised her right hand. "Sure as a seashell in the shade."

"That sounds pretty darn sure," said Theo.

She smiled up at him. "Really? I just made it up."

Theo blinked. It wasn't like Ridley to smile much. "How are we going to get in if they cannot hear us?"

"*How are we going to get in?*" Carter echoed in mock disbelief. "Have you forgotten about the talents of my lovely cousin, Leila Vernon?"

Leila already had her lockpicks out and was going to town on the contraption just below the doorknob. "This is a simple one." Within seconds, the door was open a crack and the music spilled out into the hall, all trumpets and clarinets and snare drums and the crackle-snap of a record spinning on a turntable.

"Forgive me, Leila!" Theo exclaimed. "I should have known better."

Leila winked, pushing the door open to reveal an enormous room with high ceilings. Tall windows let in the blinding morning light. Mirrors covered practically every surface except for the ceiling and the floor. There was a silver-colored couch off in a corner with a reflective table in front of it. The smell of coffee rose up from a silver set sitting in its center. A mirrored side table stood nearby, on which a record player was spinning a wide black disc.

Reflected in all the shiny surfaces were four people, each dressed in a different plaid pattern: purple, orange, green, and yellow. There was a tall, thin gentleman with jet-black hair sticking out from underneath a straw hat. And a woman with perfect blond pin curls wearing a gown that twirled when she turned. And the twins, Olly and Izzy.

The Goldens were dancing all together!

The other Misfits watched as Mrs. Golden led her husband around the spacious wooden floor, dipping and swinging him. Mr. Golden took all of it in stride, as if he was prepared for every surprise she threw at him. The twins mirrored their parents, trying to keep up with the improvisation and doing an *almost* perfect job. The music grew to a crescendo, and the four suddenly turned toward the Misfits and formed a line. They burst into a sharply choreographed tap dance, their feet moving like lightning, their arms swinging, their fingers splayed. The movements became a blur, until the music hit its final chord and the family slid onto their knees, spreading their arms and wearing dazzling smiles.

The Misfits burst into applause. What a greeting!

The Goldens held their pose a moment longer before collapsing into a wheezing, laughing pile on the floor. Theo felt a pang of envy at their easy dynamic. His family would never be able to pull off anything silly like that, nor would they want to. But then he remembered all his siblings' various talents, and he wondered what would happen if they did let loose a bit. Would family dinners be happier? Less tense?

Olly and Izzy jumped to their feet, then helped

their parents stand too. "Mom, Dad, meet the Magic Misfits!" said Izzy.

"Our best friends!" said Olly.

Mr. Golden frowned. "I thought your mother and I were your best friends!"

"No, you're our best *parents*!" said Izzy.

Mrs. Golden patted Izzy's head. "Thank you, darling. You two are our best *kids*!"

"We're your *only* kids," said Olly.

"Good thing you're the best, then," said Mr. Golden with a wink and a nod. He turned to the group in the doorway. "Welcome, Magic Misfits, to our humble-bumble abode. I'd ask you to pull up a seat but, well... we don't have any chairs!"

"My husband is just being silly," said Mrs. Golden. "We clear the floor every morning for our family dance practice."

"You do *that* every morning?" asked Ridley, her jaw dropping.

Mrs. Golden pressed one of the mirrored walls, and a large panel popped open. Inside was a collection of stools and ottomans and chairs. "Please come in. We've heard so much about you. Make yourselves comfortable. I have biscuits baking in the kitchen. Is anybody hungry?"

"Of course they're hungry," said Olly.

"Hungry for fun!" added Izzy.

"And *biscuits*, I hope," said Mr. Golden. "Because that's all we have." He followed his wife through a doorway and disappeared.

"Sorry for barging in," said Leila.

"We did knock," added Carter.

"Even I'll admit that routine was ridiculously amazing," said Ridley. "But please don't tell me it was the reason you called us up here."

"It wasn't the *only* reason," said Izzy. "Go on, Olly. Show them."

Olly did a cartwheel.

"No, not that," said Izzy. "The other thing."

Olly threw himself into a back handspring.

"Not that either," Izzy pressed. "The thing in the closet. The thing that's super important."

"More important than gymnastics?"

"Enough performing!" yelled Ridley in frustration. "Would you just show us already?" She pounded her fists on her wheelchair armrests for emphasis, accidentally sending a sudden spray of water from a secret compartment right into Olly's eyes.

Wiping his face but keeping his smile, Olly reached into the closet and took out a rolled-up piece of paper. Izzy held the top as Olly pulled down the bottom, revealing a full-size marquee poster. "We snagged one from the auditorium office downstairs," said Izzy, growing serious for what felt like the first time ever. "The hotel is putting these up today. Does it look familiar?"

On the poster was a picture of a man with wide eyes behind large circular spectacles. His brown hair was parted down the middle, revealing eyebrows that were raised in surprise. His face was trim and clean-shaven, and he wore a striped suit with a polka-dot necktie.

Beside him was a ventriloquist's dummy. The dummy's hair was also parted down the middle, and its thick eyebrows were darting downward in a menacing way. Pink blotches covered the doll's cheeks. He was dressed in a dark suit, white shirt, and puffy red bow tie. Formal, yet a tad frightening.

The header at the top of the poster read: THE GRAND OAK RESORT PRESENTS ~ WENDEL WHISPERS AND HIS DARLING DUMMY, DARLING DANIEL.

At the bottom of the poster were more words: OR, DARLING DANIEL AND HIS DUMMY, WENDEL WHISPERS!

Also: NOW APPEARING AT THE GRAND THEATER!

And finally: BAGFUL'S METRIC MIMICS PRODUCTIONS.

"Which part is meant to look familiar?" asked Theo, confused.

"I can guess," said Carter. "Izzy asked me to bring this." He opened his satchel and pulled out a picture frame. The Misfits crowded in for a closer look. Inside was a photograph of Mr. Vernon's old magic club, the

Emerald Ring, when they were young. Dante Vernon and Lyle Locke were chuckling together. Bobby Boscowitz was leaning in with a sly grin, and Sandra Santos sat clutching her crystal ball. On the far left, hidden in shadow, was the person they now knew to be Kalagan, the mesmerist who was causing all kinds of trouble in Mineral Wells (and who knows where else).

One final member sat between Sandra and Kalagan: a boy holding a dummy. A boy whose brown hair was parted down the middle, whose wire spectacles were large and round, whose eyebrows were lifted in sweet surprise, as if he had been caught off guard by the camera's flash.

"That's him!" said Ridley. "The man on the poster is the boy from the picture!"

"And look," added Theo. "The dummy is the same as well."

Leila gulped. "The ventriloquist from the Emerald Ring is coming here?"

"Why?" Carter asked. "Why would he come here?"

Theo was afraid he knew the answer.

SIX

"Wendel Whispers will be performing here starting sometime in the next few days," said Olly, not noticing Theo's uneasy expression. "He has a lot of shows scheduled. Maybe even through the end of the summer! At least that's the word around the Grand Oak."

"He's supposed to be really popular," said Izzy. She scrunched her nose. "Even more popular than us."

"And that's saying a lot," said Olly.

"No," said Izzy. "*This* is saying 'a lot.'" She paused, then said, "*A...lot!*"

Another angry spray shot out of Ridley's wheelchair.

"But is it really the boy from the Emerald Ring?" asked Leila. "Because if it is—"

"It means trouble," Theo concluded.

"Big trouble," said Carter.

"Bosso-bonus trouble," Leila added.

"Sandra-sized trouble," said Ridley.

"Kalagan-crazy trouble," said Theo. "Wendel Whispers is up to something."

"And we've got to figure out what," said Carter.

Olly and Izzy gave each other a high five. The poster dropped from their hands, fell to the floor, and rolled up tightly. Theo pulled his violin bow out of his pants pocket and pointed it at the rolled poster, which lifted from the floor as if by invisible hands. It floated to Ridley, who grabbed it and put it in her wheelchair for safekeeping. "This Wendel person is working with Kalagan—I'm certain of that," she said.

"We were thinking the same thing," Olly exclaimed.

"So, what do we do?" asked Carter.

"Let's confront him!" Leila blurted out. "Ask him straight to his face what he's up to."

Ridley shook her head. "I'm all for being blunt, but let's think this through. The ventriloquist could simply deny knowing what we're talking about, and then go about his dastardly plan anyway."

"Remember what Mr. Vernon said at the train station?" asked Theo. "We have to be prepared for all sorts of circumstances."

"Exactly," said Carter. "We need to gather evidence. See what he's up to. It's the only way we can beat this Whispers person. Him *and* Kalagan."

"And the dummy!" said Olly.

"Who are you calling a dummy?" Izzy goaded him.

"I'm calling the dummy a dummy. Who did you think?"

"Nobody, ya dummy."

"So, what, we become spies?" Leila interrupted.

"Exactly!" said Izzy, always ready for a change of subject. "I have a fake mustache I can wear."

"I have a fake nose!" said Olly.

"I have fake teeth!"

"I have fake horns!"

Theo spoke up. "I think we should continue practicing for the talent show, and keep our ears open a little wider."

"We have fake ears too!" Izzy went on.

Theo ignored them. "We find the ventriloquist.

Follow him secretly. We pick up clues. We spy, but not in any obvious way. We prepare for different outcomes, just like Mr. Vernon suggested, so that when we figure out what Mr. Whispers has planned, we will know exactly what to do."

"Agreed," said Ridley.

"Agreed!" chirped the rest of the Misfits.

"Agreed!" Mr. and Mrs. Golden cheered from the kitchen doorway. "What are we agreeing to?" The Misfits turned to find the couple standing shoulder-to-shoulder in the frame, where they appeared to be stuck.

"You first," said Mr. Golden, holding a tray of steaming buttermilk biscuits.

"No, honey, I insist," said Mrs. Golden, holding a platter with a jar of jam and a ceramic butter container. "Go ahead."

"Thank you, dear!" Mr. Golden tried to wiggle away, but he managed only to wiggle in place.

"I'll help!" shouted Olly, racing across the room.

"Me too!" yelled Izzy, following her brother.

The twins each took a tray, then they turned and walked away, leaving their parents still trapped. Olly and Izzy sat down on the silver couch and called over to the Misfits, "Who wants breakfast?"

Despite the seriousness of the situation with Mr. Whispers, Theo almost laughed out loud. And he again felt a pang of envy that the twins and their parents all loved the same things.

Suddenly, Mr. and Mrs. Golden barreled out from the doorway, having become unstuck. Mrs. Golden fell forward into a somersault. Mr. Golden rushed toward her, and at the last moment she stood up, catching him by his hips and raising his skinny frame up over her head, spinning slowly in place.

"Good one, Mom!"

"Nice job, Dad!"

As Mrs. Golden lowered her husband to the floor, she bowed to the kids. "We've been working on that for weeks," she said to the Misfits. "What do you think?"

"I think they're all crazy," Ridley whispered to Theo. He held back a grin.

"I think it was stupendous," Theo replied.

✦ ✦ ✦

An hour later, Theo's heart went *thump-thump, thump-thump, thump-thump* as the wheel of the dining cart went *squeak-squeak, squeak-squeak, squeak-squeak*.

The man pushing the cart was dressed in a bellhop's

uniform, because, well, he was a bellhop. Dean was one of the oldest employees at the resort, long past the usual age of retirement, but he was still going strong. The Misfits had recruited him to help by proclaiming that they could not wait to get a peek at the hotel's next guest performer. Dean now walked several dozen feet ahead of them down the hallway. On his dining cart sat a gleaming silver platter with a mirrorlike dome atop it.

"*Psst!*" Leila called out from around the corner where the Misfits were hiding. Dean paused, tilting his head to the side but not turning. Olly and Izzy had told him that it was of utmost importance that he pretend not to know they were watching. "That's his door on the right!" Leila whispered loudly. "Number 506."

"Oh!" said Dean, turning and peering closely at the digits nailed to the hotel door. He knocked, waited, and then knocked again.

Theo crossed his arms tightly and held his breath. What if the ventriloquist had heard Leila just now? What if he answered the door and noticed them all watching? Or what if he didn't answer the door at all? Maybe he was already down in Mineral Wells, meeting with vile contacts, setting his wicked plan in motion!

But then there was a click of a latch and a squeak of hinges, and Dean stepped back. "Pardon me, sir," he said. "But we've brought—"

No, Dean! Theo thought. *Do not say "we."*

"I didn't order any food," said a voice at the door. It was a low, rumbling kind of voice, and it sent chills up Theo's neck. A tall figure stepped slightly out into the hallway. He was dressed in a white terry-cloth robe and slippers. His big round glasses glinted in the light.

"Compliments of the house," said Dean.

"*Help!*" said another voice, high-pitched and squeaky. "*Let me out of here!*" This voice sounded muffled, like it was coming from underneath the silver dome on the cart.

Dean flinched and hopped away from it.

The ventriloquist burst out laughing. "So sorry. I couldn't help myself." He lifted the dome to reveal a turkey sandwich. "I've been practicing that one for a couple weeks, and here was the perfect opportunity for me to use it. Ever seen a ventriloquist before?"

Dean smiled a crinkled grin and held his hand to his chest. "That was good. You had me going!" He started making hiccupping sounds. For a moment, Theo worried that the old man might be in trouble. But when the hiccups continued, he realized that Dean was simply laughing. "I'll have to buy a ticket to your show, Mr. Whispers." Dean gave a slight bow.

"Call me Wendel," said the ventriloquist.

Dean peered at him. "Say, have we met? You seem so familiar to me."

"Huh. It's possible. People tell me that a lot. I guess I just have a *familiar* face."

"You've visited Mineral Wells before?" Dean asked.

The Misfits tittered nervously. Leila had begged the bellhop to try to work that question into the conversation.

"A long, long time ago, yes," said Wendel Whispers. "It's amazing to me how little has changed."

"We Mineral Wellsians pride ourselves on that," said Dean. "No one here actually likes change."

"That's one thing I can't help with. Change comes to us all. It will come to Mineral Wells someday too, I'm afraid."

"What's that supposed to mean?" Carter whispered to his friends.

"Not sure," said Ridley. "It sounded pretty cryptic."

"It sounded like a threat," Leila asserted.

"Exactly," said Theo.

"Speaking of change, let me give you a tip," Wendel said, reaching into the pocket of his robe.

But Dean held up his hands. "I couldn't possibly. You're the resort's guest of honor."

"I must pay you, man!" Wendel Whispers insisted, digging around in his pocket.

Shaking his head, the bellhop stood up straighter. "But there *is* something you could do." He leaned close. "I'd sure love to see...*him*."

Theo felt his stomach drop, but he did not understand why.

"See...*who*?" asked Wendel. Quickly realizing the answer, he added, "Ah!" Then he disappeared into the room.

A second later, a new figure emerged through the doorway. The little wooden man, only about three feet tall, wore a shabby tuxedo of faded black. Brown hair parted down the middle. A puffy red bow tied underneath his mechanical jowls and pink lips. Wide eyes and bushy eyebrows with a pert, snidely turned-up nose. Theo could make out part of an arm emerging from its backside. The rest of the arm disappeared through the doorway. This was no man.

Darling Daniel's mouth clacked open and shut, and a nasally voice seemed to kazoo forth from within. "A ticket to the show, then!" said the dummy. "I'll make sure the box office knows. Dean, is it?"

The bellhop nodded, touching his name tag. "Done and done. See you around...*Dean*," the thing finished, sounding almost threatening.

"See you," Dean replied uneasily, darting a glance toward the kids.

Theo was about to breathe a sigh of relief when something terrible happened. The dummy turned its head slightly toward the Misfits, its glass eyes seeming to stare at them, as if it had known the whole time that they were hiding around the corner. Mr. Whispers then leaned his torso out of the room, and he followed his dummy's gaze.

Theo felt his body stiffen. Beside him, his friends gasped.

The puppet's hand rose and gave them a little wave. Then, in a blur of shadow, it flew backward into the room, and the door slammed shut.

Dean rushed with the cart as fast as he could back to where the Misfits stood trembling. "Was that good enough?" he wheezed at them.

"He knew we were here!" Carter said to the others.

"So what?" said the bellhop. "You're just a group of fans, right?"

"R-right," said Carter.

The twins gulped. Leila hugged herself. Ridley's knuckles were white from gripping her armrests, but no water streamed out. Instead, it pooled on the floor under her wheelchair.

"It was perfect, Dean," Leila said finally, tugging on the sleeves of her jacket, straightening the seams. She turned to her friends. "Now we need to think about what we saw and learned."

"We got to see the dummy," said Olly.

"The *creepy* dummy," Carter added.

"Hey!" said Izzy. "Who are you calling a creepy dummy?"

It was then that everyone realized this joke was going to grow old very quickly.

HOW TO...

Levitate a Bread Roll

While the Magic Misfits are on their way back down to the kitchen, now seems like a good time to teach you a food-based magic trick. Mmm...Are you feeling suddenly hungry? That's not hypnosis—that's your stomach! Go get a snack, then come back quickly so we can get on with our lesson.

WHAT YOU'LL NEED:

A fork

A small bun or roll of bread (one about the size of a hamburger bun should work well)

A table

A cloth napkin

A chair

HELPFUL HINT:

Before your show begins, you will want to set up the trick. First, stick the fork into the bun, then rest the fork's handle on the table, pointing toward your chair. Next, cover the bun and fork with the napkin. Finally, when your audience arrives, sit down in the chair.

STEPS:

1. Greet your audience cheerfully and explain that you know how to make a piece of bread float all by itself.

2. Lift the part of the napkin that is facing your audience. Show them the bread (but keep the fork covered). Say some magic words as you cover the bread again.

3. Grasp the corners of the napkin that are closest to you. At the same time, secretly take hold of the end of the fork.

4. Use the fork to make the bread bounce into the air, keeping the bun in the center of the napkin. (Make some *ooohing* and *aaahing* sounds to encourage your audience to do the same!)

Optional challenge: While holding the corners of the napkin, allow the cloth to drape toward the table. Use the fork to lift the bun partially over the top edge of the napkin. Try to bite the bun, but then make it float away from you again!

5. Using your free hand—the one that is not holding the fork—let go of one of the napkin's corners. Grasp the bun and pull it off the fork. Move your hand toward the audience, showing them the bun.

6. At the same time, move the napkin and fork back toward your chest and then drop the fork quietly into your lap.

7. Shake out the napkin as you show your audience the bread roll.

8. Take a bite...then a bow!

SEVEN

Taking the elevator back to the ground floor, the Misfits said good-bye to Dean and headed for the kitchen, Leila pushing the dining cart. Theo opened the door for her and almost walked directly into the Other Mr. Vernon.

"Whoa there!" he said, catching Theo by the shoulders.

"Poppa!" said Leila, pushing the cart to the side. She threw her arms around her father and squeezed him. He squeezed back and smiled.

"What's this I hear about my cooks making the six of

you a single turkey sandwich? That's not nearly enough food for all of you. Come. Sit. Who's hungry?"

The Misfits gathered at a small table in the corner of the kitchen as the Other Mr. Vernon rushed around, preparing finger sandwiches and a summer squash soup for them. "No crusts, Trixie!" he instructed one of his assistants. "Very good ladling, Katia," he said to the other.

When he was finally satisfied with their lunch, he joined the Misfits, and Leila told him everything they'd learned. He took the news well, but then, Theo knew that he would. The Other Mr. Vernon was always kind and supportive. He asked them only to be careful, to remain vigilant, but to stay out of Mr. Whispers's way. When the Other Mr. Vernon mentioned that *he* wanted to check in with the ventriloquist himself, Leila interrupted. "But we don't want him to know we're onto him. If he thinks we're clueless, maybe he won't be so careful, and then we can learn his plan." The Other Mr. Vernon reluctantly agreed to stay away but said he would check with Dante as soon as he called, just to make sure they had all the facts. Then he left their table and began rolling out a delicious-looking dough.

"Let's review what we know," said Ridley, taking out her notebook and pencil. "Whispers is staying in room 506." She jotted down some notes.

"He told Dean that this is not the first time he has been to Mineral Wells," said Carter.

"Obviously," answered Ridley with a scowl. "He was a member of the Emerald Ring, remember?"

Theo shook his head. "We cannot be sure yet. This is the point of our spying, no? To learn the facts without making assumptions?"

"The reason we're watching him at all is because we *know* he was a member of Vernon's old magic club," said Ridley. She pointed to Carter's satchel, and Carter pulled out the photo. "I mean, that's him, isn't it?"

Theo breathed out through his nose. He adored Ridley and her fierce loyalty, but he hated when she treated other people like they were stupid. "That is what we are trying to find out." He glanced around the table and realized that everyone was staring strangely at Ridley and him. Arguing was unusual for them. "Mr. Vernon was adamant that we think like magicians, that we seek out all possible outcomes. One of those outcomes could be that Wendel Whispers is *not* the boy from the picture."

This seemed to do the trick. Something clicked in Ridley's head, and she wrote down what he had said.

A yelp bleated from behind them. Trixie and Katia had been tending to the dining tray Dean had used to bring the turkey sandwich to Mr. Whispers. When they had lifted the dome, a little doll about eight inches in height was sitting on the silver platter.

Theo instantly recognized it. He rushed over and picked it up. "Darling Daniel," he announced to the Misfits.

Ridley held out her hand, asking to see the doll. Theo brought it over. "But this isn't the actual dummy," Ridley said. "This is a replica. A smaller version of the original." The Misfits passed it around.

"Gives me the willies," said Katia, shuddering. She and Trixie moved the cart away from the kids and went back to work. The Other Mr. Vernon was too focused on his dough to notice.

"How'd it get under the dome?" Carter whispered.

"You should know," said Ridley. "You're the one who's so good at making things vanish and then reappear."

"It proves that Mr. Whispers knew we were watching from the hallway," Theo said.

"So, he gave us...a doll?" asked Leila.

"Maybe he wanted to make us laugh," Izzy said nervously, her eyes wide.

"Maybe he wanted to scare us," said Olly with a shiver.

"Or he wanted to warn us not to get too close," Theo added, taking the doll from Carter. The head appeared to be made of wood. The dummy's features—his eyes, his jaw, his hair—were merely painted on, as was his big red bow tie. A string emerged from inside the jacket on the back, a loop tied at the end. Theo pulled the loop, and something inside the doll began to whirr.

A tinny voice peeped, "*Now you see me!*"

The Misfits glanced at one another around the table, stunned, as though someone had stolen their voices from them.

After a few seconds, Carter said, "Let's just give it back."

"How?" asked Ridley. "Do we knock on Mr. Whispers's door and say, *Thanks but no thanks*?"

"I say we keep it," said Leila. "We can show it to my dad when he gets home."

But who knows when that will be? thought Theo. *And who knows what the ventriloquist has planned for us before that happens?*

✹ ✹ ✹

Later, the group headed down the winding road back toward the center of town. "Despite everything else," Leila said, "we need to rehearse again for the talent show. To iron out the wrinkles."

"Right," Carter agreed. "Theo's grand finale needs to be cleaned up."

"I thought we were settled on Leila's act," said Theo uncertainly.

"It's worth discussing," said Ridley. "We've got to end with something really unforgettable."

"I still think we should finish with our juggling act," said Olly.

"Yeah!" said Izzy. "There's nothing more impressive than when we juggle twelve hard-boiled eggs."

"Except when we eat them!" Olly skipped and then tumbled into a pratfall.

"No way, you guys," said Ridley. She had shoved Darling Daniel into a pouch at the back of her chair so no one would have to look at it. "Our act is a *magic* show, remember? Juggling doesn't even compare."

"Tell that to the eggs," Olly whispered with a grin as he stood up again.

Clouds were rolling in, blocking out the blue of the summer sky. From the distance, there came a rumble of thunder. The Misfits had just made it to the red-and-white-striped awning of the barbershop when the sky opened up and poured buckets onto Mineral Wells.

As they huddled together, trying to stay dry, Leila

pointed to the barbershop window and yelled out, "Holy cannoli, Carter! I knew you were good at making things vanish and appear, but this is truly impressive. I didn't even see you slip into that shop!" The Misfits followed Leila's finger to the barber's chair closest to the window, where the Darling Daniel doll was sitting slightly slumped and staring directly at them.

Carter's jaw dropped. "But I didn't—"

"It's not the same doll," said Ridley, pulling *their* doll out from her pouch.

The group went inside. The barber glanced up from his customer, a young gentleman who did not appear to need a haircut, and said to them, "Have a seat. I'll be with you shortly."

"We are not looking for a trim, sir," said Theo. "Can you tell us where you got that doll?" Theo pointed at the chair near the window.

"Huh," said the barber. "Not sure. Some kid must have left him." He went back to his customer, lathering the young man's chin and neck with a frothy cream.

Theo strolled to the doll and picked it up. His friends watched him as if he were handling a stick of dynamite. The doll looked the same as the one they had found on the dining cart—eight inches tall, big wooden head with painted features, custom-made tuxedo. A looped string came out of its back. Theo stuck his finger through and pulled. There was the familiar whirring sound, followed by the tinny nasal squeak of a voice. This time it said, *"Made of wood but filled with laughs!"*

The young man in the barber's chair turned his frothy chin to the group and said, "Hey, I've heard that voice before."

"Where?" Theo asked urgently.

The young man peered closer. "My mother found a little doll just like that this morning at the bottom of one of her grocery bags when she got home. I pulled the string, and it said…something like *that*." He pointed at the doll. "What a funny thing. It appeared out of nowhere. *Like magic*."

"There's a ventriloquist scheduled to do some shows at the resort," said Carter. "These dolls look like his dummy."

"My brother and I live up there," Izzy told the young man.

"Maybe you've heard of us," Olly added. "The Golden twins? We do a floor show in the lobby every Tuesday and Th—"

Ridley coughed in Olly's direction and shut him up. "May I ask what you're going to do with that doll?" she said to the barber. "I mean, you wouldn't mind terribly if *we* kept it?"

The barber shook his head. "It goes into the lost-and-found box. What if its owner comes back?" He whipped out a straight razor and began to remove the shaving cream from the young man's throat.

"I have a feeling that's not going to happen," Ridley whispered to the group. "What a waste." Then she raised an eyebrow and nodded at Carter.

Carter's face turned fuchsia. He mouthed, *I don't steal!*

Leila let out a chuckle that sounded slightly forced. "Okay, friends! It's stopped raining now. Time for us to get to work!" Theo took that as his cue to place the Daniel doll back onto the barber's chair near the window.

As soon as everyone was outside, Leila hugged her arms across her chest. "Mr. Whispers only showed up this morning. How'd he have time to leave the dolls around town?"

"Maybe he has a crew," said Carter, who still looked a bit red in the face.

"Just like Bosso," Ridley started.

"Just like Sandra," Theo finished.

They all glanced around the town green. People who had ducked under awnings and into doorways to hide from the downpour were starting to emerge again. Sunlight was breaking through the clouds.

"Look!" Olly cried out, pointing at the gazebo. "There's another one!"

The group rushed across the street. Olly catapulted up the gazebo steps and snatched another stray doll from the floor. When he pulled the string, the tinny voice echoed, *"Escape your boring lives with Darling Daniel!"*

"It's like they're multiplying," said Izzy. "A plague of dummies!" She frowned. "Plagues are never good, are they?"

"Not really," Olly responded. "I prefer musicals!"

Ridley grabbed the doll from Olly. "I don't trust this thing." She wheeled over to the railing and raised the doll over her head.

"Stop!" shouted Theo, coming up behind her. "It will break."

Ridley turned to him. "Exactly my plan, buddy. I want to see what's making it tick."

"But if you break it open, you might destroy the

mechanism that allows it to speak. How will you test it, then?"

Ridley frowned. "I guess I'll have to dissect it carefully when I get home instead."

"But this one is ours!" said Olly. "I'm the one who noticed it."

Disappointed, Ridley handed it back. "Fine. I still have the one from the hotel."

"Thank you," Izzy said, wiping her brow in mock relief. "He's sensitive about his toys."

"I am not!" Olly tucked the doll into his jacket pocket. "I'm just sensitive in general," he stated proudly.

One of the gazebo steps creaked. Theo whirled around to find Emily Meridian coming up behind them. Relieved, he could not hold back a smile.

"I see you guys have found another new friend." She nodded at the doll poking out of Olly's pocket.

"Hey there, Emily!" said Leila, giving the girl a hug.

Theo wished he could hug Emily too. Instead, he shook her hand. She smiled, and a warmth tickled up Theo's neck.

"You've seen them too?" asked Carter.

"Oh yeah," said Emily. "They're all over the place."

Ridley crossed her arms. "Wendel Whispers is up to no good."

"Is that some kind of code phrase for your magic club?" Emily asked.

Theo laughed. "Wendel Whispers is a ventriloquist, the new act up at the resort. Darling Daniel is his dummy, and these dolls are replicas of him. We believe they are part of his scheme."

"The resort ventriloquist has a scheme?" Emily looked as if she was trying to suppress a grin.

"He's working for Kalagan," snapped Ridley. "Of course he has a scheme."

"We are not certain about that yet," said Theo. "We need to explore all the options, remember, Ridley? Like Mr. Vernon said."

"What if the dolls are like a misdirection?" Carter asked. "Does the ventriloquist want us to look in one direction while he's sneaking in others?"

The group glanced around the town green. But they did not spot Wendel Whispers (sneaking or otherwise).

"I see the magic shop is closed for the day," Emily went on, changing the subject.

"We'll open again as soon as my dad gets back from his last-minute business trip," said Leila.

"Why don't you all come by the music shop?" Emily suggested. Theo noticed she was looking right at him as she said it. "Have some lemonade. I told my dad about you last night, and he really wants to say hi."

"Thanks," said Ridley, a fake smile smeared across her face. "But we have to practice for the talent show. Some other t—"

"I'd like some lemonade," said Theo. Ridley's jaw dropped, as if she could not believe that he had defied her.

A pang flickered in Theo's rib cage. What was the harm in a little lemonade?

"Me too," said Leila quickly. "After that walk down from the resort, my gullet's kind of dry."

Carter shrugged and stepped between Emily and Ridley. "We have time, I guess. Just for a bit."

Ridley huffed but then eased back in her chair. "Fine. Just for a bit."

EIGHT

The music shop was only a block and a half from
the park, in a row of stone houses on Main Street.
A sharply pitched tin roof slanted up to the sky
just over the second-floor windows. Black shutters
complemented the panes. Certain stones in the wall
had been painted bright colors. Chartreuse. Mauve.
Cerulean. Coquelicot. Smaragdine. (No, those are
not the names of mythical dragons....They are real
colors! Go look them up if you feel the need! I shall
wait....Welcome back. You DO look a bit wiser!) The
shop's front window was decorated with a gold-leaf

script that read MERIDIAN'S MUSIC ~ TOOLS TO HELP YOU MAKE SOME NOISE.

A mechanism was triggered as Emily opened the door, and a music box chimed a brief ragtime tune when the Magic Misfits strolled in. Inside Meridian's Music, the walls were packed with hanging instruments. Guitars, violins, and cellos. Trumpets, trombones, and tubas. Xylophones, drum kits, a couple of pianos, and even some intricate gothic-looking pump organs.

At a counter on the far side of the store, Theo could see a trim man dressed in a brown tweed suit, and as the chime ended, the man glanced up from a gadget with which he had been tinkering. His head was bald, and a long salt-and-pepper beard grew from his cheeks and chin all the way down to his shirt collar.

"Hey, Pops!" said Emily. "These are the kids I was telling you about. The magicians from down the street."

"Ah! Hello there, *magicians*," he said with

a smile. "As you've probably already gathered, I am Emily's father, Mick Meridian. But you can call me Mick."

The Misfits each introduced themselves, and Mick politely shook their hands until he came to "Theo Stein-Meyer!"

"Hello there, Mr. Meridian. Uh, I mean, Mick. Very nice to see you again."

"It's been too long, Theo. Please give your parents my best." He reached out and squeezed Theo's shoulder as if they were old friends, or even long-lost family members. Given how many instruments and how much sheet music the Stein-Meyers had purchased at the shop, Theo was not surprised. To the others, Mick added, "I've always loved magic. But I've never been very good at it. Perhaps you'll be kind enough to give us a show?"

"Right now?" asked Leila.

"Why not?"

Carter shrugged. "We *do* need to rehearse."

Ridley shifted her wheels. "I don't think we're ready for a real audience just yet."

"But you were practicing in the park only yesterday," said Emily. "Everyone was watching."

"It can't hurt," Leila said to her friends. "Can it?"

"But we don't have everything we need," said Ridley.

"We should have enough," said Carter, patting his satchel.

Theo peered at Mick Meridian, who looked amused. "Give us a few minutes to set up," said Theo.

"Not a problem," answered Mick. "Let us know when you're ready."

The Magic Misfits got ready, then went through their program. The twins started, making jokes and contorting their bodies in shocking ways. Next came Carter, who made his own head disappear. Ridley peeled the banana and revealed the surprise inside. Theo played his violin, making a handkerchief dance since he had left the teddy bear at home, and this time, at the end, he caught it. Finally, Leila reenacted the burglary scene from the magic shop, tying up the others while Theo accompanied with a classical solo.

The Misfits took a bow, and Mick and Emily clapped, but only politely. Theo felt his face grow hot. He glanced at the others, who looked similarly disappointed at the lackluster response. Mick cleared his throat uncomfortably, then said, "The best part is, you still have time to spruce it up!"

If it was meant to be a compliment, it certainly did not feel like one. Leo's words from the previous evening sprang into Theo's head. Was he wasting his time with these tricks? If the Magic Misfits were not good enough to impress even a local business owner and his daughter, maybe they were not good enough to win the Mineral Wells Talent Show.

"I thought it was great," said Emily. "You guys have a good chance at winning. I'm sure of it."

Ridley whispered to Leila, "Is *that* really going to be the finale?"

Leila looked hurt but did not answer.

Carter turned his back on the small audience and chimed in, "Leila's been working really hard—"

But then Mick clapped his hands together. "Tut-tut!" he said. "I did not intend to create any tension. Your show is going to blow them away. Truly. You just need to practice."

Olly and Izzy bowed, then rolled forward and fell to the floor, pretending to be unconscious. Ridley, Leila, and Carter began to whisper with one another about their tricks. Theo ignored them, moving toward the counter.

"It's been a long time, Theo," said Mick. "I would

have thought a musician with talent such as yours would have been more curious about the wonders I keep hidden here at Meridian's Music."

"I adore music," said Theo. "But my friends and I have grown very close. *Magic* is the thing that binds us."

Mick nodded. "Friends are as important as family. I'm happy that Emily finally worked up the courage to say hello to you. To all of you." Her eyes went wide, and suddenly, she found the floor to be very interesting.

"Courage?" Theo echoed. He had imagined that Emily Meridian was practically pulsing with courage. "But yesterday, she took down a bully in less than three moves."

"Did she?" Mick glanced at his daughter. Wearing a slight smile, Emily shrugged. "I'm impressed."

"I thought you had lots of friends, Emily," said Theo.

"Appearances can be deceiving," she answered, pursing her lips.

Mortified, Theo quickly added, "I did not mean to—"

"It's okay." Emily held up her hand. "No offense taken."

"Maybe..." Theo found himself suddenly trembling. "Maybe you would consider hanging out with the Magic Misfits sometime?"

"Yeah," said Olly, appearing beside Theo as if from nowhere.

"Definitely," said Izzy, appearing on his other side as if from *another* nowhere.

"We love new people," said Olly. "We barely know any kids up at the resort."

"Most of them come for a few days or a week and then disappear back to their ordinary lives."

When Mick turned away, Theo whispered, "Emily, you could help us keep an eye on Wendel Whis—"

"*Theo*," Ridley practically yelled out. Theo turned to find her motioning for him to zip his lips.

Theo flinched. "But she already knows...." Ridley raised an eyebrow, and he knew enough to not continue.

Leila stepped toward the counter, keeping her voice low. Thankfully, Mick was busying himself with his project again. "I think Emily would have a great time helping us spy on the ventriloquist. We're going to sneak around the resort tomorrow and use our skills to—"

Carter spoke up. "*To do secret things*. Right, Leila?" He glanced at Ridley, who threw him a smile.

Now it was Leila's turn to flinch. Carter and Ridley were side by side, as if commanders in an army, making moves to build a wall against potential threats.

Theo felt a tingling in his fingers, like static electricity building up. There must be some way to release it. It was not like the Misfits to disagree so much.

"I'm busy tomorrow anyway," Emily answered. "But thanks for the invitation." She glanced at Theo and Leila and Olly and Izzy, refusing to meet the gazes of Carter and Ridley. Everyone was quiet for an awkward moment. Then another. Finally, Emily asked, "So, is anyone still in the mood for lemonade?"

✶ ✶ ✶

Afterward, Olly and Izzy bounded up the street toward the resort, and Carter and Leila strolled back to the magic shop to check on the animals. The sun was beginning to reach toward the horizon, and Theo didn't want to break his promise to his mother.

"Walk me home first?" asked Ridley once they had said good-bye to the others.

For the first time ever, Theo wanted to answer *no*.

She had treated Emily badly. But he would not handle Ridley the same way. No matter how poorly she behaved, she had been his closest friend for what seemed like forever.

They rounded the corner and headed up the block toward Ridley's street. After a few moments of quiet, Ridley finally asked him, "Why do you want to hang out with that Emily girl so much? She's not even interested in magic."

"Do people have to like magic in order to be friends with us?" he asked. "We all found each other because we felt like misfits. How could we push someone away simply because she is not exactly like us? It would be hypocritical, no?"

Ridley sighed. "I'm sorry," she said. "I didn't think about that. I just wanted—"

"To protect us," Theo finished. "I know."

Ridley's cheeks colored. "I'm not a mean person," she added. "I just care about the people who are *already* in my life."

"But look at Carter. You were worried about him when he showed up at the Vernons', and he has turned into one of our closest friends."

Ridley didn't speak for a while, then said, "I guess I'm a little like those people who Dean was talking about earlier today. The Mineral Wellsians who don't like things to change."

Theo laughed. "This is coming from someone who lives for making everyday objects transform?" He pulled out his magic bow and touched it to the pouch at the back of Ridley's chair. Lifting his arm, he caused a banana to fly up and land in her lap.

"That's not the same thing, and you know it." She raised the banana to her nose and made it seem to disappear up inside her nostrils. She moved to pull the banana out of her ear, but instead handed him back a cucumber.

"You are going to have to teach me how to do that one day."

They had nearly reached Ridley's house on the corner. It was an elaborate yellow-and-purple Queen Anne Victorian. Its scalloped wooden shingles reminded Theo of fish scales, its turreted roof a lizard's horns. To Theo, the Larsen home was all animal—wild—just like Ridley. A light was on in a window upstairs, where her mother was most likely working on another of her popular romance novels.

"And you are going to have to teach me how that bow of yours works," she answered.

"Hmmmph," said Theo, squinting at her. "Touché."

✷ ✷ ✷

At home, Theo set the table without incident, and his family sat together, talking about how they had spent their day. Gio and Fio had taken a canoe across Wells Pond. Cleo and Leo had visited the falls and then hiked up into the hills near the resort, stumbling upon the old ice caverns that breathed out cold air, even on the hottest summer days. His siblings' tales made Theo wonder if he had spent too much of the summer indoors, hiding inside that windowless room at the rear of Vernon's Magic Shop. He thought about the tension among his friends, about the talent show, about Mr. Whispers, and even about Emily Meridian.

When his father asked Theo about his own day, Theo considered telling his family about the ventriloquist's arrival, the multiple dolls appearing, and the Misfits' desire to uncover the villain's secret plans. Instead, he told them that he had visited the music shop in town.

"The music shop?" Fio exclaimed. "How very

sensible." Everyone smiled at him, as if they were proud that he was finally getting himself back on track. Only yesterday, this reaction might have caused him to tense up. But now, he returned their smiles.

It feels good to be called sensible by people who love you.

NINE

Wendel Whispers was to begin rehearsals at the resort the next morning. So after the sun rose, Theo dressed himself, fed the doves, and practiced his violin for his father. Then he packed his violin case with a box of crackers and a bottle of apple juice (as well as his instrument) and headed out to meet his friends.

Theo, Ridley, Carter, and Leila discovered Olly and Izzy waiting outside the wide doors of the Grand Theater.

"Did anyone see you?" Carter asked the twins.

"Only a few guests," said Olly.

"And some of the staff," said Izzy. "But we stayed out of Mr. Whispers's way. In fact, we followed him down from his room, keeping just out of sight. He's been in the auditorium with the stage manager and crew ever since."

"Are you sure?" asked Carter.

"As sure as a seashell in a sheepskin!" said Olly.

"That sounds pretty sure," said Leila.

"Yes, it does," said Izzy, pulling from her jacket pocket a small scallop shell wrapped in what looked like a sheepskin coat.

"Did you *make* that?" asked Theo.

"We were hoping someone would give us a chance to use it," Izzy answered. "So, thank you, Carter. Very much!"

"Speaking of making things," Ridley began, "there's something you all need to see." She removed a parcel wrapped in cloth from the pouch at the back of her chair. She unwrapped it to reveal the feet of a Darling Daniel doll. Slowly, slowly, she pulled off the rest of the covering, until she reached the doll's shoulders. Then, with a flourish, she revealed its head—except there wasn't one!

Leila gasped. Carter cringed. Theo leaned in for a closer look.

"I did some experimenting on the doll I took home yesterday," Ridley explained.

"Did you get mad at it or something?" asked Olly.

Ridley shook her head. "I found this hidden inside the head." She opened her palm and revealed a small black device with several wires sticking out of it. The others gaped in wonder. "I believe it's some sort of radio transmitter."

"Why would that have been inside the doll?" asked Leila.

Ridley raised an eyebrow. "Why do you think?"

"The ventriloquist wants his own radio show?" Carter suggested.

Ridley blinked. "This isn't the kind of device that broadcasts radio. This one is used to transmit to a home device, so that someone can listen secretly to—and maybe even record—conversations."

Theo inhaled a deep, nervous breath. "Do you think Kalagan is behind this?"

"It would make sense," said Ridley. "If Wendel is the boy from the Emerald Ring photograph, then that would make him the third member of Vernon's old club to show up in Mineral Wells just this summer. What if these radio transmitters are the reason he's come back? To plant them where we'll be? To spy on us?"

"To help *Kalagan* spy on us," Leila added.

"But these dolls have been showing up all around the village," said Carter. "If the devices are inside all the dolls, it would mean that they're spying on the entire town."

The temperature of the theater lobby seemed to drop by several degrees.

"Which means it's imperative that we learn more about Wendel Whispers as soon as possible," said Ridley. "We must spy back." She pointed toward the theater doors. "I say we break into groups so we can watch him rehearse from multiple angles."

"Yes!" said Carter.

"Good." Leila nodded.

"What are we waiting for?" asked Izzy.

"Should we tell someone about the transmitter?" asked Olly. "The police? Our parents?"

Ridley pursed her lips. "I'd suggest we wait. Remember how the sheriff was being paid off by Bosso? We don't want to alert the wrong people that we have information. It would hinder our investigation before it's begun."

Theo felt relieved that the Misfits were working together again. "We must enter the auditorium without being spotted," he said.

They split themselves into two teams—Ridley, Olly, and Izzy in one, and Leila, Carter, and Theo in the other. Ridley and the twins headed to the orchestra pit to listen in on the ventriloquist's rehearsal. Theo, Leila, and Carter snuck up to the rafters above the stage.

Theo was extra careful as he climbed the long ladder. Gripping his violin case in one hand, he slowly moved up each rung by grasping and releasing with his other hand. Carter and Leila followed behind him silently. The higher they got, the more Theo thought of his flying dreams and hoped that he would not slip;

though he was skilled at levitation during magic shows, those skills were mere illusions and would not save his life were he to misjudge the rungs.

Finally, and with great relief, Theo sprawled up onto the walkway, accidentally banging his violin case against the metal mesh of the floor. *Oh no!* he thought. Were they caught before they even started?

Luckily, Theo could see through the mesh down below, where Wendel Whispers was sitting center stage on a wooden stool, Darling Daniel perched on his lap. Neither Whispers nor the dummy had turned at the unexpected sound.

Someone in the lighting booth across the auditorium was shining a spotlight on the man, making him glow. "How's that, Mr. Whispers?" called a voice.

"You tell me!" said the ventriloquist. "You're the one who can see what it looks like!"

Theo heard Carter and Leila crawling along behind him. When they'd all taken positions to get a good look at the stage below, Theo glanced at his friends, embarrassed that he'd almost ruined their plans. But Leila just shrugged and gave him a small smile, and Carter flashed a thumbs-up. Theo let out a quiet sigh of relief.

Wendel Whispers ran through his act as the Misfits crouched, listening. Theo had to stifle laughter several times as Darling Daniel answered Wendel in an obnoxious way. He had to remind himself that they were not here to be entertained. They needed to find out what Whispers was up to.

Unfortunately, after half an hour of listening, not once had the ventriloquist mentioned a radio transmitter. (That would have been too obvious, wouldn't it, my friend?) Theo realized that the Misfits would have to come up with a different plan to deal with the dolls.

Suddenly, Darling Daniel looked up at the ventriloquist and said, "Seems to me it's time for an afternoon snack. Whaddaya say, boss?"

"I say you don't have teeth, Daniel," the ventriloquist replied.

"Stick your finger in my mouth and say that again!" the dummy said, a warning in his voice.

"All right, all right. Don't get your bow tie in a twist. Let's take a break, please!" he called up to the lighting booth. Whispers then picked up the dummy and headed out the auditorium doors.

As the room grew quiet, Theo turned to Carter and Leila. "What do you guys think so far?"

"I think he's pretty funny," said Leila. "That dummy of his has quite a mouth on him."

"I've heard worse," said Carter, rolling his eyes. "My uncle used to curse up a storm."

"And yet, you are so polite." Theo smiled.

"I will never take after Uncle Sly."

Leila squeezed Carter's shoulder. Something secret passed between them. Theo knew that they had grown closer ever since they learned they were cousins. They were essentially siblings now.

Theo again felt jealous. His siblings insisted only on giving him advice. He certainly couldn't share his love of magic with anyone in his family the way Carter and Leila could with each other.

As if someone were reading his mind, Theo suddenly heard whispering from below. "His parents have been giving him a hard time. But it's only gotten worse since his brothers and sisters came home." Were they talking about *him*? "It's like they've all ganged up on him. And I think his performances have suffered." Theo's cheeks flushed as he turned to Carter and Leila, who were staring back at him in baffled horror. "Is that Ridley?" he asked them.

"It can't be," said Carter.

"I'm sure she doesn't mean it in a bad way," Leila answered.

Theo flinched. "Are you saying you agree with her?" he whispered. "*My magic* is suffering?"

Leila shook her head vehemently. "Not at all!"

"I just think we need to come up with something better for the finale than those stupid birds of his," Ridley went on.

"And Leila's rope trick," added Olly. "It feels so tired."

"Yes!" said Izzy. "I mean, haven't we seen it all before?"

Now it was Leila's turn to blush.

Theo felt a knot rising in his esophagus. Why were they saying these things? Even if they believed them, now was not the time.

"And don't get me started on Carter," Ridley went on. "That headless gimmick was *so* obvious...."

Carter lifted his pencil and began to tap on the railing overhead. Theo's eyes went wide, as he wondered why his friend was making so much noise, but then he noticed the pattern and understood. The tapping was the Morse code that the Misfits had been learning all summer. Deciphering the message in his head, Theo nodded. Leila too.

Stop talking. We can hear you. Whispers will too if he comes back.

But before the other group could answer, the spotlight blinked out and the auditorium was thrown into complete darkness. A door slammed shut and they heard the sound of it locking.

"What happened?" asked Theo.

Carter and Leila were only dim shapes beside him. Leila said, "If I were to guess, I'd say rehearsal is over."

"Do you think Mr. Whispers knew we were listening?" Carter asked.

"Who knows?" said Theo.

They waited in the dark for a few minutes before feeling their way slowly down the ladder and out the back door to the loading dock.

"Where do we find the others?" Carter asked, squinting in the bright light.

"I am not sure I even want to," Theo muttered, remembering Ridley's criticism.

"Let's go around to the lobby of the theater," Leila suggested, forcing a smile. "I'll bet we'll find them there."

But the auditorium's lobby was empty, and Theo felt a pit open in his chest, near where the clump of dirt had hit him two days ago. Though he was angry at his friends, he hoped they were not in trouble— trouble in Mineral Wells had the potential to be devastating.

"Look," said Leila, rushing toward a wide architectural column in the center of the room. She bent down and picked up an object.

Another Darling Daniel doll.

"Do you think Mr. Whispers left it for us?" asked Carter.

Theo and Leila did not answer. Instead, Theo held his finger to his lips and then glanced around the cavernous lobby. He could not shake the feeling that someone was watching.

Or listening.

TEN

I'll let you in on a secret to begin this next chapter, as it won't remain a secret for long (alas, secrets never do). The reason Theo felt like someone was watching and listening...

...was because someone *was* watching and listening. *Two* someones, in fact!

"Here you are!" Olly shouted, appearing from behind the column.

Carter yelped and jumped back.

"And there you go!" said Izzy, mirroring her brother on the opposite side of the column.

"How do you do that?" Leila asked.

Izzy shrugged. "Do what?"

Leila shook her head. "Never mind." With a quick look around the column, she added, "Ridley's not going to surprise us now, is she?"

Olly's usual smile dropped off his face. (The sight was so jarring, my friend, that you should be grateful you were not there. I, for one, am still shuddering at the image.) "Ridley left," he said.

"She *left*?" Carter echoed. "Where'd she go?"

Theo waved his hands at the group to tell them to *stop talking*, then pointed at the doll. He motioned for Leila to put it back on the floor and then for everyone to follow him to the other side of the room. "Keep your voices down," he said.

"She called her mother to come pick her up." Izzy pointed through the doorway toward the hotel lobby. "We asked if we could wait with her outside, but she pretty much told us to shove off. She looked upset."

She *was upset?* Theo thought. *But we are the ones who should be angry.* He clenched his violin case strap. "Without saying good-bye?" he asked. "Was she not feeling well?"

Izzy and Olly gave each other an odd glance, as if they did not wish to share the answer.

"You guys are acting weird," Carter said. "What's wrong?"

"Ridley heard what you guys were saying in the auditorium," said Olly.

Izzy nodded. "Yeah, your voices were coming through the air vents into the orchestra pit."

Carter and Leila looked to Theo. "And what exactly were *we* saying?" Leila asked.

There was no humor in Olly's next comment. "I think you should talk to Ridley about that."

This sent chills across Theo's skin. He ran toward the resort's lobby, needing to locate Ridley before her mother arrived. He raced through the crowds of people, stumbling toward the front entrance. Dean scrambled to open the door for him. "Thank you," Theo murmured, scanning the wide driveway in front of the main building.

Ridley was nowhere to be found.

But then he glimpsed the tail end of a familiar car, turning just out of the driveway and onto the main road back to town. It was Mrs. Larsen's mint-green Plymouth. Ridley was slumped in the back seat, and when she noticed him, she ducked her head further.

Footfalls came up quickly behind him. "What happened?" asked Leila.

"I was too late," said Theo, trying to catch his breath, just now realizing how fast he had run.

"At least she's with her mom," said Carter. "If she's feeling sick—"

"Ridley never calls her mom when she feels sick," Theo said, cutting Carter off. "She thinks it is better to tough it out." He faced the twins. "Please tell us what you heard in the auditorium!"

"We could," said Olly, "but then we'd have to kill you."

"Lay off the jokes," said Carter. "Can't you see he's upset?"

Izzy tugged on her brother's elbow. "Come on, Olly. We have to go feed the mice."

"Yeah, I think the Magic Misfits should take the rest of the day off, especially after what you said about the Golden family," Olly said. And with that, the twins gave an angry pirouette and disappeared through the resort's revolving door.

Theo flinched. "Wait, we said *what* about the Golden family?"

"I'm confused," said Leila.

"Someone wants us to be," Carter answered. He pulled out a deck of cards and began to shuffle them, as if that might help him sort out a problem in his head.

Theo felt for the magic bow that was folded inside his pant leg. He wished he could levitate himself and fly away from here.

Leila led the boys back inside, and Theo asked to use the phone at the concierge desk. Enough time had passed for him to call Ridley at home.

Eventually, someone answered. "Yes?"

"Hello, Mrs. Larsen," said Theo. "May I please speak with Ridley?"

"Theo," she said. "I don't know if it's a good idea right now."

Ridley's words from the auditorium hummed in his memory. *His performances have suffered. Those stupid birds.* And then the twins saying that they had heard him bad-mouthing *them*!

Anger flashed, but Theo tamped it down. "It is a matter of great importance," he managed. "Please."

Seconds later, Ridley's voice came through the phone. "What do you want?"

"I want to find out what is going on with you," he said, forcing the tremble out of his voice. "The twins told us that you were upset about something you heard us say."

"So, you're calling to apologize."

"Apologize for what?"

"Theo," Ridley growled, sounding like she might transform into a tigress. "You *know* what."

"I really do not."

"I heard you!" she exploded. "You told Carter my tricks are boring compared to the rest of the Misfits!

Olly, Izzy, and I heard it all through the vents in the auditorium!"

Theo was speechless. She was not making sense. He turned to find Carter and Leila behind him, looking concerned. He shook his head.

"I do not know who you heard through the vents, but it was not any of us."

Ridley paused. "What do you mean?"

"I promise you I never said such a thing to Carter. Or to anyone."

"I heard you!"

"You heard *someone*," he whispered. "But it was not me."

Ridley was quiet for some time. Then she said, "Fine."

"Do you believe me?" he asked.

"I mean...I have to, don't I? You're my best friend."

"We heard something in the auditorium too," he said. "Carter, Leila, and I heard you and the twins saying that my doves are stupid. That none of us should perform the finale during the talent show. But that *you* should."

Ridley scoffed. "I never said that! And neither did the twins."

"I am glad," Theo said, relieved that Ridley seemed to be calming down. "But this means someone wants us to *think* that we have been criticizing one another."

Ridley gasped. "Mr. Whispers."

"You think that the ventriloquist—"

"Wants us to fight with each other? Yes. I think exactly that."

"Can ventriloquists do that?" Theo asked, glancing at Carter and Leila. They looked like they were beginning to understand. "Sound like other people, I mean. I thought they only sat on stage with dummies and talked through their teeth."

"Ventriloquists can throw their voices," Carter said grimly. "Like in the hallway with Dean—making his voice sound like it was coming from underneath the serving dome."

"And if he can do that," said Leila, "with enough practice, he can probably also imitate anyone he likes."

"Then *this* is Wendel Whispers's plan," Ridley spoke up. Theo held out the phone so the others could hear. "He knew we were there. And he made us hear things that would upset us."

"But why?" asked Leila. "What would he get out of *being mean*?"

"The important thing is," Carter said, "we're onto him."

Ridley answered from the receiver. "We're onto him, sure," she said. "But right now he knows more about us than we know about him. And we need to stop that plan in its tracks. I say we start collecting as many of those dolls from around town as we can. That way there's no more listening in on us."

"And no more listening in on the rest of the town," said Leila. The others nodded in agreement.

Ridley sighed. "Ugh, I'm sorry I left you guys there."

"Maybe that was his plan," said Carter. "To split us apart. It worked."

A chill surged through Theo's veins. "We have to remember what Mr. Vernon said to us at the train station." *One day, something will fall inevitably out of place. Do not be caught unaware. Think things through. And try to keep control away from those who would wrest it from you.*

"It was good advice," said Carter.

"It always is," Leila agreed.

"I feel really bad," Ridley peeped. "Should I come back to the resort?"

"Yes, let's start tracking down the Darling Daniel dolls," said Leila. "We've already found another one in the theater lobby. Let's do some snooping around the resort."

"You can if you like, but I...I should get home," said Theo. "I need to practice my violin." He was not sure this was even true. What he did know was that after a morning with so much fighting and anger, he needed a break.

"But what about the dolls?" Leila asked. Carter crossed his arms, looking worried. Ridley was silent.

"The way today is going, I am sure to pass some on my way home."

ELEVEN

It was the first time Theo had ever ventured out from the resort by himself.

The long road was steep and winding, and every sharp turn made him realize how disorienting it felt without his friends to keep him company. Home seemed so far away. He could not shake the idea that there was some truth to what he had heard while hiding over the stage.

Were his friends doubting his talent?

Should he doubt as well?

Then he wondered: Was all this even important

anymore? After Ridley's discovery of the transmitter, maybe questions about talent needed to take a back seat.

With the summer sun beating down on his shoulders, Theo found himself craving the lemonade Emily had offered to the group yesterday. Usually his tuxedos made him feel as though he was important, and his jackets and slacks were necessary because they contained many hiding places for his magical supplies. But was all that worth his current discomfort?

He slipped out of his jacket and slung it over his shoulder. For the first time, Theo wondered if he should consider a different sort of outfit.

He soon came upon someone walking in front of him in the road. Someone with long blond hair. Someone dressed in a black cotton shirt, capri pants, and ballet flats.

"Emily?" he called out, and the girl turned around.

"Theo!" She waved. "I was *just* thinking about you."

Theo made his way down the hill to where she was waiting for him. "I was thinking about you too! How odd."

Emily's cheeks turned red. "I mean, I was thinking about *all* of you. The Magic Misfits."

Now it was Theo's turn to be embarrassed. "Well, I was thinking of your lemonade from yesterday," he added, as if that might correct his mistake.

"Come to the music shop. We still have a great big jar in the icebox."

Theo considered it, but was too exhausted from the events of the day. "Thank you, but I have to get home. Another time?"

Emily shrugged. "Sure thing."

"Were you just up at the resort?" he asked.

Emily shook her head. "I was walking that way to see if I could find you all, but then..." She pointed at her feet. "I realized I wasn't wearing the right shoes for this hike. So I turned back. I forgot how steep it is."

Theo wiped sweat from his forehead, nodding in agreement. They continued onward toward the town.

"I lied just now," Emily added a moment later. "I'm sorry. It wasn't my shoes that made me turn back. I...got worried that Ridley would yell at me if I showed up."

"That is understandable," Theo said with a nod. "She can be blunt."

"How did everything go this morning? Did you get some good spying in?" she asked with a wry grin.

"We did some spying. Though I doubt anyone would have called it *good*."

Emily chuckled. "Oh, you're too hard on yourself. I'm sure—"

"No, really," Theo interrupted. "It was bad." He did not feel like he should explain why. Ridley's discovery of the transmitter was a secret at the moment.

"No one ever said being a sneak was easy," she answered.

Theo laughed. "Do you think we are being creepy? Sneaking around? Tracking a man and his dummy?"

"Well, when you put it like that..." She chuckled. "I guess I don't know what to think. With the rumors about the Magic Misfits floating around Mineral Wells all summer, who knows what to believe?"

Theo laughed again, but now he felt rather uncomfortable. "What kinds of rumors?"

As the two strolled, Emily told Theo the stories of the Magic Misfits that she had overheard from customers in the music shop. As she spoke, he added a few corrections, filled in gaps, and made her promise not to tell anyone else. Emily looked enraptured, as if she could not believe that adventures such as these were possible in their sleepy small town.

"That's amazing," she concluded. "You guys are practically superheroes!"

Theo's skin tingled. "Superheroes?" he echoed. "Hardly." His flying dreams blinked into his head. Emily had just nailed one of his greatest wishes right on the noggin.

His muscles twitched as he considered what it meant when you wanted to hold someone's hand. The feeling made him want to learn how to tap-dance like the Golden twins. But he would not dare do so in front of Emily.

"Are you *sure* you don't want to come to the music shop?" she asked. "I bet my dad would be happy to see you again. Sometimes I think he stays cooped up in that place a little too much."

"My siblings are only in town for a little while longer before they scatter back to their lives all around the world. I should spend at least *some* time with them."

"All around the world?" she echoed. "What do they do?"

"They are musicians. Like me. Only they are professionals. My oldest brother, Leo, says I need to stop playing around with magic and focus on my violin."

"My mother can be similar," Emily went on. "She's always on me about my grades, even though I never get anything lower than a B. Living up to other people's expectations is exhausting."

"Agreed."

For some reason, the faces of his friends popped into Theo's mind. Then he realized that their expectations of him were sometimes exhausting too.

Emily smiled and said, "Will you show me how you levitate things?"

"A magician never reveals his secrets," Theo answered, removing the magic bow from the pocket of his pants. "But a magician also never turns down a request to perform." He ran ahead of her, then turned back. "Stay right there," he said. She paused in the middle of the road.

He angled his body toward her in just the right position, then raised his bow over his head. "This is taxing. I might need you to catch me."

"Catch you?" Emily answered worriedly.

Theo began to mutter some magical words to himself. *"Sim...sala...bim!"* And with that, he appeared to rise up several inches from the gravel road and hover there. Emily shrieked as he managed to bring his heels back down to earth. Theo bowed deeply.

"That was freaky!" she proclaimed. "What the heck were those words you said?"

"*Sim sala bim*?" Theo mentioned. "Oh, it's just something that Mr. Vernon is always reciting. The words must have some mystical powers, because they almost always work." He grinned, slipping the bow back into his pocket.

"Maybe if I say them to my mom, she'll stop fighting with my dad all the time."

"I thought you said that they were not—"

"Oh, they're still married," Emily answered quickly. "But Mom decided to take a job up north a few years ago to help support the music shop. I'm supposed to split my time between them. Summers with Dad. School with Mom up north. It's weird."

Theo suddenly felt bad for complaining about his own family, who were all still very much together. "I am sorry."

"I'm used to it at this point. I don't let it get me down."

"Good!" said Theo. "And if you ever *do* feel down, just let me know, and I shall levitate you back up again!"

Emily smiled. She took his hand. It happened so fast that he almost yanked it away. "Thanks, Theo."

Her palm was warm against his own. He had to force himself to keep breathing. "You're—" His voice was gritty, so he cleared his throat. "You're welcome."

Once they reached the town green, they said goodbye and parted ways. Theo turned the corner onto his street and realized that he felt like he was floating.

And this time, no *sim sala bim* was required.

* * *

When Theo reached the stone path in front of his home, he heard music echoing from the backyard—a melody as buoyant as a rainbow. Curious, he walked around to find his siblings gathered on the patio with their parents. They were each playing an instrument, creating a jazzy tune that twisted like starlings in an evening sky.

Theo smiled and took out his violin. As he pulled the bow against the strings, his sister Fiona trilled her voice with happiness, welcoming him. His other siblings' instruments grew quieter, wordlessly pushing Theo to take the lead.

He closed his eyes as the music rose and fell, almost as if he and his siblings were playing a game together. Theo would slow the tempo and the others would follow, only for him to change the melody on them. They played and played, getting louder and faster until the family burst into a frenzied finale, followed by a long silence.

Theo opened his eyes to the sudden sound of clapping.

"Wonderful," said his mother. "Just wonderful."

"You all make us very proud," added his father.

"Say," said Leo. "Has anyone else heard about the Mineral Wells Talent Show?"

"I've seen some signs," Cleo piped up.

"We should go," Gio suggested.

"Not only go!" said Fiona. "We should play in it."

"We would win," said Leo. "Not to toot our own horns, but there's more talent in this family than in all of Mineral Wells combined."

Theo's smile disappeared. "The Magic Misfits are competing," he said quietly. "We have been practicing for a while now."

He saw a look pass between his parents.

"But, Theo, you're so good," said Cleo.

"*We're* all so good, especially together," added Gio.

"If you don't realize that music is your calling, I don't know what to tell you," Leo chimed in.

Theo wanted to say that they were wrong, that magic was as much his calling as music. He thought briefly of levitating himself, if only to see the looks of amazement on their faces. But he knew he would just as likely see boredom and disappointment.

"Come on, Theo, help us win the talent show!" Fiona cajoled him.

"Let me think about it," he answered, surprising everyone—most of all himself.

TWELVE

The next day, Theo's brothers and sisters asked him to join them on a hike around one of the lakes at the base of the cliffs. Afterward, they went swimming and ate a picnic lunch, and in the afternoon they raced across the water in two separate canoes, Theo's team winning by no more than the length of his violin bow.

These outings continued all week, and Theo invited Emily Meridian to join the family on one of their treks. He wanted to ask to hold her hand again, but the looks his brothers and sisters were giving him and Emily were embarrassing enough. Still, it felt good to have Emily as part of their group. She was easygoing and friendly.

She also reported that more and more of the Darling Daniel dolls advertising Wendel Whispers's show were appearing around town, and if you found one, it felt like you had won a prize. People were placing them in windowsills and in the rear windshields of their cars. Children clung to them from atop their parents' shoulders. The dolls were everywhere, watching the town from high in tree branches and from low behind bushes.

It was downright creepy, and Theo knew the time had come to reconvene with the Magic Misfits. Almost a week after he had last seen his friends, he arrived at the Golden family's suite to find a stack of Darling Daniel dolls piled in a corner of the mirrored living room.

"You have been busy," Theo stated. The others looked up at him in surprise. He *had* missed several practice sessions for the talent show....

"We have been *extremely* busy," Ridley answered. "Carter and Leila found several dolls just outside the magic shop. Olly and Izzy located a bunch in the palm pots in the lounge, and a couple underneath the tables in the dining room. I gathered a few from the grocery store, and last night, I cracked open their heads and found a radio transmitter in each."

"Listen to this, Theo," said Olly. He lifted two dolls from the pile and pulled their strings. One of them said, "*You will not believe your eyes and ears.*" The other said, "*No time like now to get your tickets.*"

"Are these messages to promote the ventriloquist's show?" asked Theo.

"We think they might be a code," Carter said grimly.

Ridley nodded. "The villains could be using the devices to communicate with one another."

"Or the messages might just be simple advertisements," said Leila hopefully.

"I doubt it," Theo replied.

"Either way, these few dolls we've collected won't be enough to stop Kalagan," Ridley added. "We were all just talking about how we have to get the dolls away from the people who've already found them."

"Problem is, *I don't steal*," said Carter, crossing his arms.

Ridley shook her head. "Can someone please explain that *this* wouldn't be stealing? We'll be collecting dangerous items before they can hurt people."

"And the Misfits have the skills to do it," said Leila. "Come on, Carter. It could even be fun."

Carter pursed his lips, unconvinced. "Should we at least practice for the talent show first?"

"If that's what it takes to make you say yes," Ridley quipped. "I have some more thoughts about the fin—"

"I do not think we should wait to gather the dolls," Theo interrupted, afraid of what would happen if they started arguing about their grand finale again. "There seem to be more Darling Daniels around town every day."

"That's true," Leila quickly agreed. "We can practice more later." Everyone seemed relieved at the suggestion.

Olly and Izzy had seen the resort manager, Mr. Arnold, bring one of the Daniel dolls into his office earlier that day, so the Misfits headed downstairs to the lobby. Who knew what secrets the doll (or rather, who was listening *through* the doll) might learn from someone with access to so much private information? But in order to get to the Darling Daniel, the Misfits would need to distract what seemed like hundreds of people milling about.

Luckily for them, dear reader, *hundreds of people* is the

perfect-sized crowd for an audience.

After making their way across the lobby to the Grand Oak Resort's famous life-sized taxidermy bear, complete with a black top hat on its head, Izzy climbed onto Olly's shoulders, and Theo used the bear to steady himself as he climbed on top of the twins. He then waved his violin bow, calling out to the crowd. "Good morning! Welcome to the Grand Oak Resort!"

Several heads turned to look, and out of the corner of his eye, Theo saw Carter, Leila, and Ridley slide quietly behind a large potted plant right next to Mr. Arnold's office.

"My name is Theo Stein-Meyer! Below me is Izzy Golden!" Izzy

held out her arms. "And below her is her twin brother, Olly Golden!" Olly did a tiny tap dance, shaking his partners above. "We have come to impress and entertain you with a mini magic show. Watch closely...." He waved his violin bow over the bear's top hat, which suddenly lifted off its fuzzy crown. Theo moved his arm, and the hat seemed to float wherever he pointed. The crowd applauded.

Next, Theo made the hat spin through the air until it landed with a *plop* on Izzy's head, the brim slipping down over her eyes. The crowd laughed and clapped even louder, more heads turning to watch the show. The bear's hat then flew up off Izzy's head, as if by itself, and somersaulted to land on Olly's head below. All the while, Theo was waving his bow, wearing a look of intense concentration.

Olly reached up for the hat and held it out before himself. Theo leaned down slightly and waved his bow above the hat's opening. To everyone's surprise, two little mice floated up and out of the hat and hovered in the air, squeaking nervously.

"Meet Ozzy and Illy!" shouted Izzy and Olly. "Our magical mice assistants!"

Several people in the audience squealed. Others

laughed. Theo could see that Carter, Leila, and Ridley were still hidden behind the potted plant, so he waved the bow toward the crowd, and the mice began to float straight toward the audience.

Several guests scrambled to get out of the way, and a few people shrieked. Children tried to catch the floating mice as their parents whipped them away, and there were cries of outrage as people began knocking into one another.

Right on cue, Mr. Arnold's office door flew open and hit the wall with a *wham*! He was wearing his standard white suit, and his face was as red as ever. Seeing the twins and Theo stacked one on top of the other, he called out to them, "What's going on out here?"

"Impromptu magic show, boss," said Olly, lowering himself to his knees. "Good for business." Izzy held up her hands to Theo, who slid off her shoulders. She followed him down, dropping from Olly. The mice plopped onto the floor and scurried into a crevice near the stairs.

"Were those *mice*?" Mr. Arnold asked, his face aghast. "In the Grand Oak Resort?"

"Don't worry, sir," Olly replied. "They'll find their way back to our place."

"Yes," said Izzy. "They're the smartest mice we could find."

Mr. Arnold's eyes bulged. He turned to address the flustered resort guests.

Theo glanced toward the office, which Carter, Ridley, and Leila had just slipped silently inside. A moment later, they waved for him to follow. Theo made sure that the twins were keeping Mr. Arnold busy, and then he dashed inside as well.

Right away, Theo could see the Darling Daniel doll on the very top shelf behind the manager's desk. "We can't reach it," Leila whispered.

"Give me a moment," Theo replied, climbing up onto the back of the desk chair. Carter and Leila held his legs as Ridley kept watch at the door. Theo wondered if his friends expected him to levitate the doll to bring it down, but in this case, the solution was much simpler. He grinned as he swung his bow, pushing the doll right off the shelf. Carter reached out with one hand and caught it before it could hit the floor.

"Come on!" Ridley said with a wave, peeking out the crack in the door. "The twins are running out of obnoxious material!"

A few seconds later, Theo, Carter, Leila, and Ridley

strolled and rolled nonchalantly past the taxidermy bear, just out of view of Mr. Arnold, with their newest acquisition secreted away in Ridley's pouch. "Ahem!" Ridley said, coughing loudly.

Not missing a beat, Olly and Izzy smiled at Mr. Arnold, gave a bow to the remainder of their lobby audience, and then skedaddled into the crowd.

HOW TO...

Make a Card Rise from Your Palm

I wish I could teach you how to make a pair of field mice float, but not everyone keeps a spare pair of mice around. So let us instead make a playing card lift up and spin in the palm of your hand! This one will take some preparation, but with practice, you will have your friends' eyes popping out of their sockets.

WHAT YOU'LL NEED:

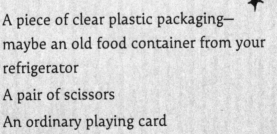

A piece of clear plastic packaging—maybe an old food container from your refrigerator

A pair of scissors

An ordinary playing card

A glue dot (these are soft and clear, and you should be able to find them wherever you purchase arts and crafts supplies)

TO PREPARE:

1. With an adult's help, cut out a thin rectangular strip of clear plastic. Make sure it is just a bit smaller than the length of the playing card.

2. Place the glue dot in the center of the card, then press the plastic strip against it, making sure the ends of the strip do not extend beyond the card's edges.

STEPS:

1. Find the right spot on the palm of your hand so that you can grab only the ends of the plastic piece. Try fitting one end against the base of your thumb and the other just inside your ring or pinky finger.

 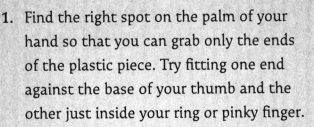

2. Squeezing the ends of the plastic slightly, allow the card to lift carefully away from your palm.

3. For an added effect, use your other hand to twist one end of the card slightly toward you, so that when you release it and then squeeze the plastic, the card will appear to spin as it rises mysteriously from your palm.

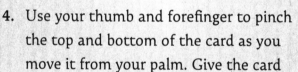

4. Use your thumb and forefinger to pinch the top and bottom of the card as you move it from your palm. Give the card a little spin for one last flourish before tucking it safely away.

5. As always, take a bow! You're amazing at this (or you will be once you practice, practice, practice...)!

THIRTEEN

Over the next few days, Theo and his friends searched for more Darling Daniel dolls. Their hunt led them to the old mill by the river, to the nursery school playground, to Molly Freundlich's Quilting Museum, and to the movie theater off Main Street, where they performed for small audiences just long enough to distract the holders of the dolls.

It felt like old times, and Theo was glad the tension from their adventure in the auditorium spying on Wendel Whispers had evaporated. The Misfits had even agreed on a finale for their act in the talent show: the re-creation of the frown clown battle.

They also concluded that the Darling Daniel dolls had been set up to speak no more than six messages, the last of which said *"Look no farther than the Grand Oak Resort."* If not for the transmitter inside each doll, it really did seem to Theo that the dolls' messages were simply a promotion for Wendel Whispers's show.

On Wednesday, the Misfits decided to put their hunt for the ventriloquist's dolls on pause and head over to the fairgrounds for the first day of the Mineral Wells Hot Air Balloon Festival. Theo and Ridley arrived at the front gate and waited for the others.

"It's been too long since we all just had some fun," said Ridley.

"Really?" Theo said, raising his eyebrows. "I have never thought of you as someone who enjoys fun."

Ridley flinched. "Of course I do. What kid doesn't?" She pulled out a stick of gum, unwrapped the silver foil, and held it up for Theo to see. Printed on the pink piece were the words *Some Fun*. Theo smiled. Ridley always had something up her sleeve. She popped the gum into her mouth and began to chew. A few minutes later, she stuck out her tongue at him playfully. Printed on her tongue, somehow, were those same words. *Some Fun.* It almost looked like a tattoo.

Before Theo could applaud the trick, a voice spoke in his ear: "Where are all the balloons?" He spun to find Olly and Izzy Golden dressed in their finest matching plaid rompers.

"They have not started filling them yet," Theo answered.

"They must be waiting for the hot air to arrive," said Olly.

"And here you are!" Izzy quipped, poking his shoulder.

Olly rolled his eyes so hard he did a backflip.

"Who's ready for some real-life levitation?" Leila asked, walking up with Carter.

Theo smiled and raised his bow in the air. "I enjoy levitation in all forms."

The Misfits moved through the gates together. Inside the grounds, there were a dozen carts arranged in the center of a large field. Long swaths of fabric stretched away from each, and team members rushed around holding up pieces of the cloth as air rushed inside. Slowly the balloons began to form subtle shapes. Some were spherical, but there was one that looked like a famous cartoon mouse, and another that was turning into a dragon. Each balloon had a distinctive pattern too. There were rainbow stripes, harlequin diamonds, white stars on a shimmery navy blue, pink hearts on a green background. One purple balloon was even illustrated with a white dove of peace carrying a sprig of laurel in its beak.

It was amazing to watch them rise. The Misfits sat in wonder as all twelve of the balloons grew to their full height, some over a hundred feet tall.

Suddenly, Ridley gasped. "What's wrong?" asked Carter. Ridley pointed toward one of the concession-stand lines. At the counter, Wendel Whispers had just ordered a giant hot dog.

"What do we do?" asked Leila.

"We track him," said Ridley.

"Why?" asked Carter. "To watch him eat his hot dog?"

"You never know what we might learn," said Theo.

"From a *hot dog*?" Carter repeated.

Ridley threw her hands in the air. "From his movements. From his behavior. From whoever he talks to. *Everything.*"

Wendel turned toward the field of balloons, finishing his meal, and the Misfits flinched away from one another, worried that he might catch them staring. The man nodded to himself, as if he had made a decision. Then he pulled out a little book from his rear pocket and jotted something down.

A clue! thought Theo.

Wendel strolled away from the food vendor and across the midway to a booth with a giant sign that read PURCHASE RIDE TICKETS HERE!

"Come on," said Ridley. "Let's follow him."

The Misfits broke into groups of two and then split up to avoid detection, each pair taking a different route toward the ventriloquist. Theo went with Leila.

"Should we buy tickets too?" he asked once they were closer to the booth. "To make it look like we are not merely hanging about?"

"Good idea," said Leila.

Wendel stood several people ahead of them in line. Theo could see Carter off in the distance with Olly. Ridley and Izzy were peering at Theo and Leila from behind the ticket booth. Everyone looked worried. Theo remembered Mr. Vernon's advice. *Plan for an out.* Right now, if something were to go wrong, if Wendel Whispers were to turn around and charge them, they would have nowhere to go.

The line was moving quickly. Theo watched Whispers buy a single ticket, and before he knew it, he and Leila had stepped forward for their own.

Leila tugged at Theo's elbow. "He went this way," she said. Wendel was headed toward the balloon with the white stars and navy background. Staff near the balloons directed the crowd, shouting over the blasts from the kerosene burners. "How many in your group? This way! No, that way!"

It was all very confusing. Theo and Leila handed over their tickets and were shoved forward—right into the balloon with the stars. They found themselves staring at the back of Mr. Whispers, who was looking out over the fairgrounds, chuckling to himself. Had he *wanted* the kids to follow him on board? Theo wondered.

The balloon's pilot directed a staff member to drop the sandbags that were hanging off the sides of the basket, and the balloon began to rise up from the ground. Theo gulped. *Now we* really *don't have an out*, he thought.

There were five passengers, not including the pilot. Everyone was peering out over the landscape except for Theo and Leila, who stood as close to the center of the basket as possible. "If he moves, we move," Theo whispered. "Do not let him see us."

"What if he already has?"

Theo did not want to think what would happen if the ventriloquist spotted them. Would he dare to toss them overboard? It was scary, but they also had a unique opportunity.

Wendel Whispers's notebook peeked out from the man's back pocket. Theo nudged Leila, nodding at it. What if there was something important inside—something that might help the Misfits figure out how to stop him from listening in on them, and the rest of the town, through the Darling Daniel dolls?

Theo pulled out his magical violin bow, careful to avoid knocking his arm against any of the other passengers. He made the secret maneuver that would allow him to lift the notebook from Wendel's pocket, and then, very carefully, he began to raise his arm. The notebook slipped upward, inch by inch, until it dangled in the air between Theo and Leila. Wendel did not seem to notice. He was snapping photos of the surrounding landscape with a small camera. Theo grabbed the floating book and hid it behind his back. He and Leila then moved toward the opposite side of the basket.

Leila whispered, "Let's look through the book now, then put it back before we land."

FOURTEEN

Oh no!

I was so involved in telling Theo's story that I nearly forgot about our unlucky chapter: thirteen!

In the previous books, I managed to cross it out. Yikes!

Since I missed it last chapter, let's just skip chapter fourteen instead?

You are not superstitious anyway.

Or are you?

FIFTEEN

"What do we do?" Leila asked.

Theo shushed her. Wendel was facing them, but he did not seem to have noticed her holding the book, nor the fact that she had just dropped it. "Lovely day," they heard him say to the woman standing next to him.

"Say," replied the woman. "Aren't you..."

Theo was thankful for their conversation, which was a perfect distraction as the balloon began its descent. When they touched down, Theo and Leila forced themselves to the rear of the group so that they could look for the notebook a few extra moments.

"There!" Theo whispered, pointing. The book lay in the grass on the side of the basket opposite the exit. "How are we going to get it without someone stopping us?"

Leila reached into her pocket and pulled out a long white rope, which she quickly turned into a lasso. And with a flick of her wrist, the lasso was looped around Wendel's notebook. Leila reeled it in so quickly, Theo barely had time to worry that someone was watching.

Once he had picked up the notebook and shoved it inside his jacket, he and Leila took off toward the

fairgrounds midway. They were hiding between two tents selling cotton candy and lemonade when Theo felt someone grab his arm. "Run, Leila!" he cried.

"No, Theo, it's just Carter!" she said, relief in her voice. Carter, Ridley, Olly, and Izzy were standing behind the duo, all looking displeased.

"What were you guys thinking? That was really dangerous!" Carter said.

"He could have discovered you," Ridley agreed.

"He could have tickled you!" added Izzy.

"He could have bought you a pet peacock!" Olly said wistfully.

Theo stared at Olly, shook his head, then pulled out the ventriloquist's notebook. "But it was worth it," he said. "We finally have some intel, *real intel*, about him."

"You stole that?" asked Carter.

"We're going to give it back," said Leila, "hopefully before he notices it's gone."

"What's inside?" asked Ridley.

Taking a deep breath, Theo opened the cover. The ventriloquist's scrawl was messy and difficult to decipher. Still, he managed to read it aloud: "*Wendel Whispers's Food Journal*." He looked up, a burning sensation already blooming in his cheeks. He flipped through the first few pages. *"Breakfast: two eggs and half a cantaloupe. Midmorning snack: half a cup of fresh yogurt sprinkled with granola. Lunch: baked cod—"*

"We get the point," said Ridley. "You've found *intel* about the ventriloquist's diet."

Theo turned to the last entry in the book, where Wendel had written the words *Balloon Festival splurge: one hot dog with mustard.* "Ugh!" he said, slamming the pages closed in disgust. How could he have been so stupid? Risking their safety to simply catch a glimpse of—

"Maybe it's not just a food journal," said Leila, gesturing to Theo. He gave her the book. "Remember how my dad's business ledger was written in code?"

"Yes!" said Carter. "The code that hid the names of the members of his secret society!"

"Let me see that," Ridley said. She flipped through the pages. "I don't see any sort of pattern here. Maybe he's written secret messages by using anagrams."

"What's *anagrams*?" asked Olly, using his fingers to make air quotes.

"Obviously, the ventriloquist's *gramma* is named *Ana*," said Izzy.

Ridley sniffed, almost amused. "Anagrams are words or phrases whose letters can be used to spell other words or phrases." Izzy and Olly looked at each other, confused. "For instance, I remember an old one that goes, *The eyes, they see.*"

"See what?" asked Izzy.

"No, no," said Ridley. "Think of the letters in the words. The first part of the sentence—*the eyes*—contains the same letters as the second part of the sentence—*they see*—only they're mixed up to form *new* words."

"Oh, I see!" said Olly.

"No, *eyes* see!" Izzy quipped.

Carter peeked over Ridley's shoulder at the open notebook. "So what anagrams are in *one hot dog with mustard?*"

Huddled between the tents on the midway, the six scoured the ventriloquist's journal. Ridley wrote down some possibilities in her own notebook. Most of the anagrams sounded ridiculous.

Throw out something, Dad.

Diamonds thought tower.

Editor, shut down Gotham.

But then the Misfits discovered combinations that looked like names. Many, many names:

Seth Dartmouth Wooding.

Hedwiga Toots Thurmond.

Howard Hutting Modesto.

It soon became clear that there were just too many possibilities. "The names might be relevant," said Ridley, "*if* we've come up with the correct combinations. But the more I write down, the less likely it seems."

"That's too bad," said Olly. "I really wanted to meet Hedwiga Toots Thurmond."

"I'll bet she's a judge," said Izzy.

"Or maybe a bank robber," said Olly.

"She's probably a professional trombone player!" said Izzy. "*Toot, toot, toot!*"

"That's not what trombones sound like. Trombones go wah-*wahhhh*."

The idea of a sad trombone playing at that moment was sort of appropriate, because just then Theo heard Wendel Whispers's voice coming toward them. "I have no idea where it went," he said to someone the Misfits could not see. "It was in my pocket one minute, and the next it was gone!" They turned to find the ventriloquist out on the midway, speaking with a security guard.

Each of them froze. And when the guard pointed toward them, they froze even harder.

"Head that way," said the guard. "You'll find exactly what you're looking for."

"Follow me!" said Ridley, pushing her chair down the path between the tents.

The kids obliged, bumping into one another and scrambling to keep out of the mud. They came to the end of the row only to find themselves at a high chain-link fence. They turned to the left and raced forward.

Theo imagined the ventriloquist chasing him down—a large hand reaching for his collar, throwing him to the ground. *Where's my notebook?!* the man would demand. Theo looked over his shoulder to find Wendel's long shadow stretching out from between the tents, in the alley where the Misfits had just been hiding. "Over here!" Theo waved for everyone to follow him into a space behind a small booth.

There was just enough room for all of them to fit.

"So much for planning a way out," whispered Ridley. "What if Whispers discovers us hiding back here?"

"Quit your yammering," Carter mumbled.

Everyone gasped. Carter turned white.

"Quit my what?" Ridley asked threateningly.

"I didn't say anything," Carter answered, his pale skin blushing vibrant pink.

"Then who did?"

"I don't know, but it wasn't me!"

"You're just jealous because I'm the only one here using my brain," said Ridley. "Mr. Vernon warned us about something like this happening."

"He also told us that we need to stick together," cautioned Leila. "Remember?"

"We couldn't be any more together than this," Ridley shot back. "We're practically on top of each other."

"Shh!" Theo hushed them. Footfalls sounded from around the other side of the booth.

"Hello there," the ventriloquist said. "I'm wondering if you can help me."

Theo's stomach dropped.

Just then, someone else answered. "Sure hope I can, mister. What do you need?"

"This is the *lost-and-found*," said Wendel. "Is it not?"

Lost-and-found! The security guard had not sent Wendel to chase the Misfits—he had simply been directing the ventriloquist to this booth.

Now's our chance, Theo thought. This was the perfect opportunity for them to return the notebook, no questions asked. Ridley had already copied down everything that she needed. But how would Theo manage it?

He lifted up the canvas at the bottom of the back of the lost-and-found booth. Peering underneath, he could see several wooden crates stacked under the counter where Wendel Whispers was standing. Theo slipped his bow out from his pocket and took the notebook from Ridley's lap.

"Hey!" she snapped, but he ignored her. There was no time to argue.

"You said it was a lost notebook?" asked the teenager in the booth. Theo watched as the boy leaned down and began to dig through the wooden crates. "Can you tell me what it looks like?"

Wendel Whispers huffed. "Well, it looks like a...a notebook! What more do you need to know?"

"We need a diversion," Theo said quietly.

Olly raised his and his sister's hands. "Ready, willing, and able."

"Hurry," said Theo. "We do not need anyone discovering us."

"No problem, boss," said Izzy. She grabbed her brother's wrist, and together they skipped out from around the corner.

Soon, there was the sound of bodies colliding and someone letting out an "*Oof!*"

"Goodness gracious," said Wendel. "Are you two all right?"

Peering under the canvas, Theo could not see what the twins were doing, but the distraction was exactly what he had hoped for. Even the teenager was no longer paying attention to his booth.

Theo swung his bow underneath the flap and made the ventriloquist's notebook dance across the dirt floor. Then, with a flick of his wrist, the book jumped off the ground and landed directly inside one of the wooden crates. Theo wanted to cheer but managed to hold back. It felt like he had just won some sort of strange carnival game. In a flash, he pulled himself out from under the flap.

"So sorry," he heard Izzy proclaim. "My brother is such a klutz."

"And proud of it!" Olly answered.

Theo allowed himself a small smile. He was sure the twins were now scampering off toward the midway, leaving Wendel and the teenage attendant in baffled silence.

✦ ✦ ✦

They followed Wendel Whispers—notebook back in his pocket—at a distance all the way to the center of town. Ridley took notes every time the man stopped to talk to someone. A gentleman in a brown fedora. A young woman pushing a baby carriage filled with what looked like laundry. A couple dressed in matching denim overalls. Each person was holding a Darling Daniel doll. The ventriloquist shook the dolls' hands and pretended to be zapped by an invisible buzzer, making the people laugh.

"There are just too many dolls," Carter said. "We can't collect them all."

"It feels like all the work we've done is for nothing," said Ridley, frustrated.

"Maybe we need a new plan," Leila suggested.

"Like what?" asked Olly.

"I know!" said Izzy. "Cartwheels!" She demonstrated.

Leila shook her head. "I was thinking more along the lines of sending an anonymous letter to the *Mineral Wells Gazette* so someone will report on the radio transmitters in the dolls."

"But even if the letter is anonymous, Whispers and Kalagan will know *someone's* onto them," said Ridley.

The group fell silent. Only when the ventriloquist hopped into a cab just outside the barbershop—which Ridley also noted in her book—did Theo finally speak.

"Are we going to talk about what happened?" he asked, leading the group toward the magic shop.

"*What* what happened?" asked Olly, scrunching up his forehead.

"Back behind the lost-and-found," Theo continued. "When Carter was mean to Ridley."

"But I wasn't mean to Ridley," Carter protested. "I know you heard me say, *Quit your yammering*. I heard it too. But I swear I never said it."

"I believe you," said Leila. "We've already dealt with voices imitating us this week. Wendel Whispers was right there at the booth, doing it again."

Ridley scowled, looking unsure.

"Even if that is true, it is not the part we need to talk about," Theo said. He gave Ridley a hard look. "Ridley's answer is what makes me nervous."

"What did *I* say?"

"*You're just jealous because I'm the only one here using my brain*," Carter repeated. Ridley's cheeks turned pink, and she scowled harder.

"Can't we all just be kind to each other?" Leila asked.

"Yeah," said Carter. "We can't focus on what Whispers is doing if we keep fighting."

"And what is he doing exactly?" Ridley asked.

"Trying to *make* us fight!" Carter practically yelled. "Can't you see that it's working?"

"No way," Ridley said, opening her notebook. "His plan can't be that simple. We have all this evidence—"

"What evidence?" asked Theo. "We managed to get a glance into his food journal, which may or may not be filled with secret anagrams. I am leaning toward *not*."

Ridley's eyes widened with frustration. "We just saw him chatting with all those people around town. They could be his cronies."

"Or they might just be ordinary people who liked his show," said Leila. "Each of them had a doll."

Ridley shook her head. "So, what you're saying is that Wendel Whispers is *not* working with Kalagan?"

"I'm not saying that," Leila said. "It's just, from what we do know, he's trying to *mess* with us. Maybe it would be better if we started ignoring him."

"I don't want to take that risk. Do you?"

The Misfits were silent for a moment.

"I agree with Leila," said Carter. "I think we should cool it for a while. At least until Mr. Vernon gets back."

Theo's head felt swimmy. None of this was fair.

They should all be able to have a normal summer vacation without worrying about villains who may or may not have infiltrated their beloved town.

"You know what?" Ridley snapped. "I'm feeling pretty tired. I think I should head home."

Carter and Leila glanced worriedly at each other.

"If that's what you want," said Leila, "we understand."

"Who's we?" Ridley asked. "It's like you're all ganging up on me."

"We're not!" said Izzy.

"We would never gang up," Olly added. "We only gang *down*."

"Maybe lunch will make us feel better," Theo said. "How about we all talk later?"

"Great," said Ridley. "Theo, let's go."

Theo flinched. "I...I think I'd like to be by myself right now." He glanced at the others, trying to gauge if his response was too cruel. They only looked at him sympathetically.

"Fine," Ridley said flatly. "Olly, Izzy, want to come over?"

"*Yes!*" Izzy cheered. "I've always wanted to see where you live."

"Lead the way!" Olly added. Neither twin seemed to realize that their enthusiasm was making the rest of the Misfits cringe.

Ridley headed off toward the corner. At the last second, she turned back and glared at her friends.

No, not at her friends, Theo thought. *At* me.

SIXTEEN

"Are you okay?" Carter asked Theo.

"I think so. I just hate when Ridley gets like this."

"I know what you mean," said Carter. "When I arrived in Mineral Wells, I thought she hated my guts."

"Ridley doesn't hate anybody," said Leila. "She's just frustrated. Like the rest of us."

"You're welcome to come into the magic shop for some grub," Carter said to Theo. "We can feed Change-O and then take him out to the gazebo. He loves watching the squirrels."

Theo glanced into the darkened window of Vernon's

Magic Shop. Even though he could see rows of book-shelves, jars filled with magical doodads, and Top Hat, the rabbit, hopping aimlessly about inside, the shop seemed to have lost some luster. Without Mr. Vernon there, it felt as though a valve of its heart had stopped beating.

"Thank you," said Theo. "But I meant it when I said I would like some time alone. How about a rain check?"

"Rain-check us anytime," said Leila. "And you don't have to wait for rain either."

Theo gave her a small smile, then walked away in the opposite direction, dragging his feet.

He could not head home. No one there would understand what he was going through. And he was afraid that if he were to spend another minute with his friends, his anger would grow and expand, like a giant balloon. But there was someone else he knew he could talk to. Someone who lived only a couple of blocks away.

When he reached the music shop, the lights inside were on, so he swung the door open. Already, his pulse was quickening at the thought of seeing Emily. (Ah, dear reader. Is there anything more magical than the expectation of seeing someone who makes our hearts pitter-patter? Erm—that is...oh dear. I appear to be blushing. Please excuse me.)

Theo looked around the shop but saw no one there. Soft music was coming from the back, though, and he wandered closer to peer through a back door that was slightly cracked.

Mick Meridian was leaning over a workbench, facing away from Theo. A gramophone turned in the corner, playing a scratchy-sounding minuet. Mick swayed as he listened and fiddled with a contraption on the bench.

Theo noticed something on the back of the man's neck, something he had not seen before. A pinkish, puckered blotch of rough skin spread up from Mick's shirt collar, reaching around toward his left ear. It looked like a scar.

The door squeaked slightly as Theo leaned on it, and Mick Meridian swiveled on his stool. "Who's there?" he called out.

"Theo Stein-Meyer," Theo answered through the crack. "So sorry. I thought the store was open."

"Theo!" Mick stood and practically ran toward him. "Welcome, welcome. Of course we're open.

It's just been such a slow day, I decided to come back here and do some *specialized* work." He gestured at a shelf on the wall above the workbench. On it sat half a dozen curious devices. "Metronomes," he explained. "It's a little hobby of mine."

Theo had seen gadgets like these before. In fact, there was one sitting on the piano in his own living room. A metal pole stuck up out of the wooden base and ticked back and forth, helping musicians keep time. *Tick. Tock. Tick. Tock.* You could adjust the tempo to be slower or faster by sliding a weighted piece of metal up or down the pole.

Mick Meridian's metronomes were different from any Theo had seen before. Each one had a weight that was a different shape, like charms on a bracelet. There was a hand, a pyramid with an eye inside, a crescent moon turned on its side, and a hypnotic, swirling disk. There was a bright red apple and a burgundy heart. "You made these?" Theo asked, and Mick nodded. "They are spectacular!"

"You're kind." Mick smiled. "Now, I have a guess as to why you're here, but unfortunately, my daughter isn't around. She went to check out the hot air balloon festival down at the fairgrounds."

Theo could not stop his smile from falling away. "I was just there."

"I'm surprised you didn't run into Emily. She told me she was going to look for you."

"Really?" Theo's skin warmed. "Maybe we walked right by her."

"We?"

"I went with my friends from the magic shop."

"Ah yes, the magic shop." Mick's gaze turned inward, as if he was remembering something. "How *is* Vernon?"

"He is still away, actually. Umm, business." Theo felt strange saying it that way, as if he were lying.

Mick pressed his lips together. "But something's wrong. I can tell. Maybe not with Vernon...with your friends?" Theo said nothing but hung his head.

"Close friendships can be tricky to maintain, much

like an antique musical instrument. You can't play too hard. And there is always the risk of things beginning to corrode."

Theo felt something clench inside his chest. But then he started to talk. Slowly. About the ventriloquist at the resort and, without being specific, how the Misfits were worried that the man had a wicked card up his sleeve. He talked about Ridley and how difficult she could be. Finally, almost reluctantly, he mentioned the odd mimicry he and his friends had heard around the town—the ventriloquist throwing his voice and trying to make the Misfits fight. Theo kept the radio transmitters to himself, though, worried about what Ridley would say if he revealed that piece of information.

"I find it hard to believe that anyone could *make* a close group of friends fight," said Mick. "The tension must have been there in the first place." He drummed his fingers on the countertop. "Do you think maybe you're jealous of one another?"

"Jealous?" Theo echoed. "I never thought we were. Not until this summer. Not until the talent show."

"Maybe it would be better if you stopped trying to force the talent show. Take a break from one another for a while. Time apart can mend deep wounds."

"Maybe," said Theo. He thought of his siblings and how far they all lived from one another. Coming together over the past week had felt good, but it had taken time and effort to get there. "I will consider it."

"I hope you do," said Mick. "And music is always a good distraction."

"That too," Theo answered. "My brothers and sisters and I have started riffing in our backyard. It has been fun."

"Perfect!" Mick stood. "Tell you what. I have something for you." He waved for Theo to follow him into the back room again. Pointing at the shelf over the workbench, he said, "Pick one."

Theo's stomach dropped. "You want to give me a metronome?"

"They're not doing any good sitting back here! Pick one and use it when you and your siblings have your next jam session. My gift to you. For being so kind to Emily."

Theo scanned the shelf. The last metronome on the right caught his eye. It had a heart-shaped weight. Emily's face popped into his head as he told Mick, "That one is beautiful."

A couple of days later, Theo woke to the sound of the phone ringing. His mother knocked on his door and then opened it a crack. "Is it for me?" he asked, worried.

"It's someone named..." She glanced down at a scrap of paper. "*Ollinissy?*" She sounded confused. "They *insisted* I wake you. Is everything okay?"

Theo sighed, putting on his slippers. "I shall let you know momentarily."

Padding down to the phone in the upstairs hallway, he picked up the receiver and asked, "Olly? Izzy? What's wrong?"

The twins spoke over each other. But Theo got the gist of what they were saying. There was an emergency at the resort. He needed to come as soon as possible.

By the time Theo arrived at the Goldens' suite, the other Misfits were already there. Carter and Leila had hitched a ride with the Other Mr. Vernon. And surprisingly, Ridley had spent the night with the twins.

"Thank goodness you're here," Ridley said as he came into the living room. The furniture was all in place—there would be no morning dance practice for the Golden crew today. "We can finally get started."

She turned to the others, perched all around the room. "I motion that this meeting of the Magic Misfits begin immediately."

"Seconded," said Leila.

"Thirded," Olly and Izzy answered at the same time. "Jinx!" they both cried out. "Double-jinx!" they both yelled. "Triple—"

"Why are we here?" Theo interrupted. "Olly, Izzy, I apologize. But did someone get hurt?"

"Not yet," Ridley answered. "Thank goodness." She reached around to the back of her chair and removed a large rolled piece of paper. Theo recognized the poster for Wendel Whispers's ventriloquism show. "But someone *will* be if we don't do something."

Theo, Carter, and Leila leaned forward. Olly and Izzy already seemed to know what this was all about. They flanked Ridley's chair in support.

Ridley handed the poster to the twins, who held it up for everyone to see. Ridley pointed at the words on the bottom of the poster. "I couldn't stop thinking about what we were saying the other day. The anagrams."

Chills coursed across Theo's skin. He had enjoyed the few days away from Wendel Whispers and Kalagan.

The thought of the mystery zooming front and center again made him queasy.

Leila read it aloud: *"Bagful's Metric Mimics Productions?"*

Ridley took out her notebook and opened it. Theo could see that the pages were filled with her handwriting. "I woke up this morning with those words racing through my head. They're almost nonsensical, but not quite. I tested out the letters, rearranging them again and again. And look what I found."

She rested her finger against the page.

The final line in the notebook read *Magic Misfits crumble.*

Theo stood straight, bringing his hands to his mouth. He looked to Ridley, almost expecting her to be grinning with satisfaction, since she'd been right about the ventriloquist. But she looked just as frightened as the rest of them.

"Cripes," Carter whispered.

"There's no way this is a coincidence," said Leila, shaking her head.

"We need to confront him," Ridley asserted. "Today."

"We already know where his room is," said Izzy. "Let's go now."

Magic Misfits
Crumble !!

"Too dangerous,"
said Carter.

"We should tell Mr. and Mrs.
Golden." Theo glanced through the door
to the kitchen, but all was quiet.

"Mom and Dad left earlier to go teach classes to the
guests," Olly explained.

"Then we wait until they come back," said Theo. "I
do not think we should leave this room until they do."

"What about Dean?" Izzy asked. "Maybe he can
help us again."

Ridley rolled her eyes. "By doing what? Carrying
our luggage?"

"My poppa is downstairs in the kitchen," Leila suggested.

"And what will we tell him?" asked Ridley.

Theo glanced at the poster again. Darling Daniel's big glass eyes looked out at him, seeming to stare into his mind.

"Everything," Theo answered. "We tell him everything."

✴ ✴ ✴

In the parlor just off the dining room, the group gathered at one of the couches hidden in a nook of densely potted foliage. They kept their voices down as they explained their worries to Leila's poppa. When they finished, he said, "This is bad. This is really, really bad."

Theo grit his teeth. He had been expecting the Other Mr. Vernon to say something soothing like *There must be another explanation* or *I will take care of everything. No worrying allowed!* Instead, the man just sat there, biting his lip.

"I need to talk to Dante," he whispered to himself.

"Did Mr. Vernon ever check in with you?" Theo asked.

Carter and Leila shook their heads.

"But Poppa said that it was all right," Leila added. "That Dad can handle whatever it is he's dealing with."

"And he can," the Other Mr. Vernon asserted,

although he still looked worried. "But we need to talk to this Whispers guy today. Right now if possible."

"We cannot go up to his room," Theo pleaded. "We need to talk to him in public. He cannot do anything bad to us in front of others." *Make us* crumble, he thought.

"Spot on, Theo," said the Other Mr. Vernon. "We get him to come to us."

"How?" asked Olly.

"And where?" asked Izzy.

"And when?"

"And who?"

"This is serious," Ridley barked. The twins covered their mouths and stepped back as if out of a spotlight.

The Other Mr. Vernon nervously bit at the inside of his cheek. "The front desk has a phone. And the lobby is full of people. Getting him down here will be as easy as baking a cake." He rushed into the kitchen and returned moments later holding a thick rolling pin coated in a layer of flour.

"Baking a cake is *easy*?" asked Olly.

"It's all in the wrists." The Other Mr. Vernon then brandished the rolling pin toward the lobby. "Now—let's get rolling!"

SEVENTEEN

The taxidermy bear looked down blankly at the friends from the top of the lobby stairs. Today it was dressed in a grass skirt and a coconut top. It almost made Theo smile. But worry hung from his heart, and his mind went back to the creepy poster. Why would someone want to target the Magic Misfits? A group of kids who were merely trying to have fun, make magic, and create smiles?

"Carter and I wrote that anonymous letter to the *Gazette*," Leila whispered. "Telling them about the transmitters in the dolls. We dropped it in the mailbox this morning."

Ridley nodded. "That was the right move."

"I'm scared," said Olly. "What if the ventriloquist tries to hurt us?"

"I'm hungry," said Izzy. "What if the kitchen runs out of lemon squares before we get any?"

Theo was glad for the twins' banter. It was a good distraction. The Misfits kept their eyes on the elevator doors by the front desk, waiting for Mr. Whispers to appear.

A few minutes later, a voice boomed from behind them: "I know you!"

Turning, Theo found Wendel Whispers standing over them. He was cradling the real Darling Daniel dummy like a baby. Both were looking right at the Misfits.

Wendel had not taken the elevator to the lobby! Mr. Vernon's advice flashed through Theo's mind: *Magicians must be prepared for all sorts of outcomes.* They had missed this one for sure.

Darling Daniel's head swiveled between the Misfits, as if taking them in. "What's wrong?" he screeched. "Cat got yer tongue?"

"You two rode in the hot air balloon with me yesterday," said Wendel. He looked at Theo and Leila, whose faces flushed. Theo pressed himself backward into the love seat, expecting the man or the dummy to reach out and throttle him. Instead, Wendel smiled. "Wasn't that fun?"

"It was very pretty up there," Leila answered, her voice a squeak.

"I'm thinking of going again today," said the ventriloquist.

Darling Daniel added, "It's *my* turn to ride in the sky."

Several guests had noticed the ventriloquist, and a small audience was forming. Some of the guests were even holding Darling Daniel replicas.

"I'm sorry I left you home yesterday," Wendel told the dummy. "But you insisted you weren't feeling well."

"Only because I didn't want to eat that slop you were having for breakfast!"

"Tell a lie, deal with the consequences," Wendel stage-whispered to the dummy. Then he glanced at the Misfits and smiled again.

This time, Theo was fairly sure the smile was not

meant to be nice. He looked to the front desk, where the Other Mr. Vernon was caught up in conversation with a receptionist. Ridley moved suddenly toward the ventriloquist.

"You can quit your charade, Mr. Whispers," she said, her tone clipped.

Wendel flinched. "Excuse me?" he said, dropping all pretense of performing for the people passing through the lobby. He tried to step around Ridley, but she positioned her chair to block him. She almost ran over his toes. "Whoa," Wendel said. "A little close, don't you think?"

"We know who you work for," Ridley continued. "And we know what you two are up to."

"*Ridley*," Leila whispered urgently.

But Ridley went on. "So, you can just quit it now. We're not going to leave you alone until you pack your bags and get the heck out of Mineral Wells."

Wendel straightened his spine, rising to his full height, his pale face turning the color of the red roses in the large vase by the front door. "And just who do you think you're talking to, young lady?"

Ridley inhaled sharply as if she was about to let him have it.

"Ridley, wait!" Theo said. "The Other Mr. Vernon will help." He ran toward the desk as the confrontation continued loudly behind him. "Wendel Whispers is here!" he shouted, skidding to a stop.

The Other Mr. Vernon whirled around, then practically galloped across the room, flour puffing out behind him like a steam engine. Theo raced after him.

Olly and Izzy were now holding the poster open, and Ridley had her notebook out and was showing her anagram work to the ventriloquist. His brow was scrunched, and his mouth was a slack little O.

"I had nothing to do with that," he said. "Someone here at the hotel must have put this poster together using a very old picture of me and my dummy."

"Hello, Mr. Whispers?" the Other Mr. Vernon interjected. "I'm the chef here at the resort. I called you down to the lobby. My daughter and her friends have experienced some difficulties this summer, and we hoped you could answer a few questions."

Wendel rolled his eyes. "I can assure you, sir, that I have nothing whatsoever to do with any secret messages this young lady has discovered in my show's promotional materials. *Magic Misfits crumble*? I don't even know what a *Magic Misfit* is!"

"*We're* the Magic Misfits," said Carter, glancing at his friends. "We do magic." He snapped his fingers and a deck of cards appeared in his other hand. He fanned them out, revealing the suits and courts. Leila placed her hand on his shoulder, and he stood straighter. "And we're misfits." He brought the cards back into a pile. "And we don't believe a word that you're saying." Spreading the cards again, he revealed them all to be blank.

"I don't know what to tell you," said Wendel, unimpressed. "Where's the manager? Maybe he can settle all this."

"There's no need to involve Mr. Arnold," the Other Mr. Vernon answered. "Like I said, we just hoped to ask you some questions." He glared at the kids. "That is, if everyone would just calm down for a moment. Shall we sit?" He then shooed away what was left of the curious crowd that had gathered.

Wendel Whispers rolled his eyes again, set down Darling Daniel, then sat beside him on a love seat. Sighing, he said, "Someone please tell me what this is all about?"

Leila began. "Earlier this summer, my friends and I stopped a man named B. B. Bosso from stealing a giant diamond during a magic show here at the resort." Theo expected to see some glimmer of recognition in Wendel's eyes, but he only stared angrily at the Misfits. "Bosso was trying to pin the theft on my other dad, who owns the magic shop in town. The two of them knew each other back when they were kids. They were in a magic club just like ours. Theirs was called the Emerald Ring."

"But you know all this already," said Ridley.

"Do not deign to tell me what I know," Wendel said indignantly.

"A few weeks ago, another member of the Emerald

Ring came to town," Leila continued. "Sandra Santos, also known as the psychic Madame Esmeralda. She performed here at the Grand Oak Resort, then she and her cohorts broke into my dad's magic shop and tried to steal an important notebook."

"I'm beginning to see a pattern here," said Wendel, though he looked more bored than intrigued. "I assure you, however, that I have nothing to do with this magic shop you keep talking about. Nor with any old magic club. I don't even do magic. I'm a ventriloquist!"

"That's the thing," said Carter. "We *know* you were part of the Emerald Ring. We overheard you say that you've been to Mineral Wells before, a long time ago. We have a picture of you with the club from way back when." He flipped open his satchel and pulled out the antique framed photo. "You even have the same doll!"

"Caught red-handed," Ridley growled.

"I got Daniel out of a catalog decades ago," Wendel explained, "as did *hundreds* of aspiring ventriloquists all around the world. The model is quite common. The boy in your picture must have ordered his from the same company."

"But the boy looks just like you!" Theo said in disbelief.

"And any good magician should know that appearances are illusions." Wendel sniffed. "How many people in this country do you think have similar haircuts and comparable eyewear to the boy in this photograph? Thousands?"

"But *you're* the one who showed up here," said Ridley. "In Mineral Wells. With the same dummy. What are the chances?"

Wendel sighed. "They are low, I will admit. You do realize, however, that I was *invited* to come here. If you're all so suspicious of me, maybe you should look into who books the talent at this resort."

The Other Mr. Vernon blinked. "That's a good point."

"Besides," Wendel went on, "I can prove to you that I am not the boy in that photo." He took off his glasses and leaned toward the Misfits. "Look into my eyes."

"Don't do it!" shouted Olly, leaping in between the ventriloquist and the rest of the group.

Wendel nearly fell off the love seat. "I'm not a hypnotist!" he cried out. "I am merely asking that you notice my eye color."

"Blue," said Ridley. "So what?"

"Bright blue, to be exact." Wendel gestured to the

photo of the Emerald Ring. "The boy in your picture has brown eyes."

The Misfits went silent. "He's right," said Leila. "This boy's eyes are dark."

"That can't be," said Ridley. "We know this is you!"

"Do you have any other proof?" asked Wendel as he stood. The group was silent. The Other Mr. Vernon looked mortified.

"The creepy dolls that you made appear all around the town," Ridley barged on. "The dolls that literally everyone is carrying." She reached into the pouch behind her chair and pulled out a Daniel doll.

"Those were a hotel promotion I had nothing to do with," said Wendel. "Again. Honestly, I've never met a group of kids with such wild imaginations."

Ridley opened the compartment in the arm of her chair and removed a long screwdriver. "If it was only a promotion, then why did I find this inside?" She raised the screwdriver and brought it down, right in the center of the replica dummy's forehead. Its face split open as the entire head cracked in half, and a small electronic device spilled out into Ridley's lap. A light on its side was blinking.

"What *is* that?" said Wendel. His pink cheeks grew pale.

"A radio transmitter," Carter said grimly.

Ridley looked at the ventriloquist triumphantly. "You're no dummy, Mr. Whispers." She held up the transmitter, which was still attached to the doll's throat by a wire. She pulled the string on the doll's back, and as it spoke—*"Now you see me!"*—the blinking light grew stronger, as if the act of pulling the string charged the transmitter's battery. "You've been using these dolls to listen in on us," Ridley whispered. "To listen in on *the whole town.*"

EIGHTEEN

"Admit it," Ridley went on. "You're working for Kalagan!"

"Kalagan?" Wendel echoed. "What's a *Kalagan*?"

Carter pointed to the shadowy figure in the corner of the Emerald Ring photograph. "*This* is Kalagan. Only he's all grown up now. B. B. Bosso and Sandra Santos were working for him."

"He's a mesmerist who's obsessed with controlling people for his own gain," said Leila.

"He's a con man," said Ridley. "Pure and simple."

"A *dangerous* con man," Theo added.

Olly and Izzy put up their dukes and waggled them like boxers at the beginning of a match. "We had to fight off his goons when they attacked us at the magic shop."

A strange look came over Wendel's eyes. "You're not joking around," he said, almost to himself. He lifted the electronic device from the destroyed doll and examined it closely. Then he gave it a good yank and plucked it away from the wire. Its light went dead. "I don't want anyone listening in on me without my permission," he said quietly. He glanced around the room, as if Kalagan could have been watching even then. Theo thought it was a totally reasonable fear. "In fact, this whole thing is giving me the heebie-jeebies." He picked up his dummy and slung him over his shoulder. "Please excuse me," he said to the Other Mr. Vernon. "I can't stay here any longer."

"What do you mean?" the Other Mr. Vernon asked. "Don't you have a show tonight?"

"Not after what you all just shared with me." The man shivered. "Maybe you'll think me dramatic for wanting to leave, but I will not allow myself to be a pawn in a game. Someone at this hotel has set me up." Wendel Whispers turned on his heel and walked quickly toward the elevator. The Misfits were quiet as they watched the doors close on him and his Darling Daniel dummy, whose glassy eyes stared off at nothing.

"What do we do now?" asked Carter.

Leila tapped her chin. "Wendel made it sound like someone at the resort was responsible. Whoever put up the posters could have inserted the anagram. The Darling Daniel dolls were a hotel promotion. We need to collect the rest of them from these people." She gestured to the resort's guests. "The *Gazette* won't be able to look into our letter until at least—"

"No one's doing anything," said the Other Mr. Vernon. "At least not until I speak with Mr. Arnold. *He* should know all the employees who were involved in the making of the posters and the dolls."

"Are you sure that's safe?" Leila asked, reaching for her poppa's hand. "What if Mr. Arnold is the one responsible?"

The Other Mr. Vernon raised the wooden rolling pin. "I'm prepared," he said with a grin. He headed up the steps toward the manager's office, taking them two at a time.

Theo stood and paced. "I cannot help but think that if we had been following Mr. Vernon's advice, if we had considered *all* the paths, *all* the outcomes, we would not be in this situation. Early on, I asked us to consider that Wendel Whispers was *not* a member of the Emerald Ring. Remember?"

For a moment, they were all quiet.

"Let's not argue anymore," said Leila.

"So then how do we *make* an out for ourselves?" Carter asked. "We could sure use one."

Ridley rolled forward a couple of inches. "I suggest we write it all down. *All* the people involved. *All* that could happen. *All* the ways we could escape from danger. *All* the stuff that we're not expecting."

"How can we learn to expect what is unexpected?" Carter asked.

"Have you heard of something called using your brain?" Ridley quipped.

"Not nice, Ridley," Leila chided.

"There's no time to be nice! Something bad is coming, and it's not going to stop and wait for us to get along. We need to think. We need to fight."

"But not with each other," Leila said.

"Fine!" Carter yelled, holding his hand out for Ridley's notebook and pen. "Let's use your brain."

"Not just *my* brain," Ridley said, seeming to notice she'd gone too far. "All our brains."

"I plan on using Izzy's brain," said Olly.

Of course, Izzy began to answer, "I plan on using—"

But Theo had stopped listening. Not only was he sick of the arguing, but something on the floor near the wheel of Ridley's chair had captured his attention. It was a fragment that had fallen out of the broken doll's head, a piece of metal that looked vaguely familiar.

He bent down and palmed it just like Carter had taught him. He felt like his throat was closing up.

Because you see, dear reader, Theo knew that what

he had found on the floor was the answer the Misfits were looking for. The clue that would begin unraveling the mystery.

But he could not bring himself to share it with them.

NINETEEN

Theo told his friends that he had to head home.

Once outside, he took off, running down the winding road back to Mineral Wells faster than he had ever run before. He kept his hand pressed against his tuxedo jacket pocket, making sure he could feel the piece of metal there.

If the ventriloquist was worried enough to pack his things and leave, what did it mean for the Misfits? Mineral Wells was supposed to be their sanctuary, their haven, their home. Now it was turning into a twisted carnival maze.

He skidded to a stop on the sidewalk just outside the music shop, trying to catch his breath. When the door unexpectedly swung inward, he yelped and nearly stumbled off the curb. Emily appeared from inside, wearing a look of concern. "Theo? Are you okay? Why are you sweating? Did you run here or something?"

"May I come in? I must show you something."

Emily cocked her head and then moved aside, motioning to the stools at the rear of the store. She brought Theo a glass of lemonade, which he gulped gratefully. Afternoon sunshine angled through the window. Despite Theo's fear of what was about to happen, there was something magical about being in this beautiful place with Emily.

(My friend, I must interject—the word *magical* here means something different from the tricks that the Misfits practice. Sometimes *magical* can describe a feeling. It can be about a place, about a special object, even about a memory, good or bad. In this case, however, the feeling was about a *person*. If you haven't felt it already, I bet you will soon.)

"Where is your father?" Theo asked, finally catching his breath.

"Running an errand. He'll be back in a few minutes."

They were both quiet for a moment. Only the metronomes made any sound.

Tick, tock, tick, tock, tick, tock.

Theo wanted to shout at the devices, which seemed to be hurrying him along. He needed this moment of peace to last just a few seconds longer.

"Is this about that ventriloquist person? Did you guys figure out what he's doing in Mineral Wells?"

Theo took a deep breath, then placed the metal piece on the counter between them. "Have you ever seen something like this before?" The trinket looked like a small cog attached to a spring.

Emily froze. After a moment, she answered, "Where did you get this?"

When he finished telling her about that morning, she sat in silence for several seconds. "And what does all that have to do with a piece of metal?"

"I have only seen something like it once before," he answered. "In your father's workshop. The other day when we were chatting, I saw him building one of his metronomes. He was using pieces like this."

"It's a common attachment for moving parts. Don't the dolls' heads swivel?"

"It is not *that* common."

Emily licked her lips. "So?"

Theo tried to swallow, but even after a glass of lemonade, his throat was too dry. How should he phrase this question without hurting her feelings? "I was wondering...if maybe your father might know what it was doing inside a Darling Daniel doll that Ridley broke open."

She frowned at him, then she nodded at the front door. "Lucky you, Theo. Here he is."

Theo stood. Mick Meridian was struggling with a satchel filled with fruits and vegetables. Theo rushed over to help. "How nice to see you, my friend. Thank you!" Today Mick was wearing glasses. Big round ones.

"You're welcome," Theo whispered, noticing the large brown eyes behind the lenses.

Brown.

Not blue, like Wendel Whispers's.

Brown.

Reader, you have likely just figured out what is

going on. And I am sure you are just as aghast as Theo. But I can assure you, whatever you are feeling, it isn't magical, and it cannot be as all-consumingly sad and confused and angry as our young musician friend.

"It *is* you," Theo said sharply, taking a step backward.

"Me?" Mick asked, his expression blank.

"You are the boy from Mr. Vernon's picture. The one holding the dummy that looks like Darling Daniel." Words kept coming even though Theo knew that each one spoken nudged him closer to danger. "*You* were in the Emerald Ring. *You* did all this?"

A shadow came across Mick Meridian's gaze. He flicked his eyes to his daughter and then nodded at the front door. Emotionless, Emily stood, walked across the room, and twisted the switch over the handle, locking them all inside the music shop. Mick turned his head, revealing the puckered pink flesh that Theo had noticed the other day. The scar. It reached up nearly to the man's ear.

"Sit down, son," Mick answered, his voice surprisingly soft. "We need to talk."

"I should go." Theo tried to hold back his panic. "My mother and father—"

"Will be waiting for you when you get home."

Emily was looking at her feet. "It's okay, Theo," she said. "No one is going to hurt you."

Theo sat down on a stool, then waited for Emily to meet his eyes. "I do not understand. You *knew* your father was working for Kalagan?"

Emily's mouth opened, but no sound came out.

"Working for Kalagan?" Mick echoed. "Oh no, Theo, you have it all wrong. But...that's my fault." The shadow had passed from the man's gaze. "To answer your question, yes. I *am* the boy from Vernon's photograph. I was close friends with Dante and Lyle and Sandra and Bobby. Even Kalagan himself. But I don't work for him now. I never have and *never* will."

Theo tried to speak but his voice cracked, and nothing came out.

"I don't blame you for being confused," Mick went on. "But let me explain. You already know that I'm a craftsman. I make things."

Theo gulped, then nodded.

"I use my skills to build exquisite instruments. You've seen my beloved metronomes. But what I haven't told you—haven't told anyone besides Emily— is that *I* built the wooden dolls for the ventriloquist's show."

The questions that the Magic Misfits had raised that morning came rushing back into Theo's mind. "Who commissioned you to do it?"

"Chauncey Arnold, the resort manager," Mick answered. "We've known each other for years. He asked me to create a doll that could contain a speaking apparatus. He thought it would be a mysterious gag to leave them all around the town. To get people talking." Theo glanced at Emily, the hurt plain on his face. "Don't be upset with my daughter. I asked her to stay quiet while the resort was trying to promote the show."

"They won't need to promote it anymore, Dad," Emily answered. "Wendel Whispers is leaving Mineral Wells. Theo and his friends found something inside your dummies. Something I *know* you didn't put there."

"Radio transmitters," Theo added.

"That's...odd." Mick looked puzzled. "I knew they were going to add the speaking devices with the pull strings, but what need would there be for radio transmitters?"

"To listen to people," said Emily.

Theo pressed his palm against the counter. "People like me and Leila and Carter and Ridley. And the twins."

"Kalagan?" whispered Mick.

"We think he's here in Mineral Wells," said Emily. "Just like you feared. And he wants to hurt them." She told her father what Theo had told her—about the anagram on the poster, the secret message that was meant to scare the Magic Misfits.

Theo then reminded Mick about the voices he and his friends had been hearing around town. Voices that were trying to break them apart by sowing discord. Playing their tensions against one another. Making them angry with one another.

"I'm so sorry for all this," he said sadly. Mick squeezed Theo's shoulder.

"It is hardly your fault," Theo said. "You knew nothing of the transmitters."

"No, but...it wasn't Kalagan who was trying to break up the Misfits." Mick shook his head. "It was me."

Emily cleared her throat. When Theo glanced at her, he saw tears welling in her eyes. "And I helped him."

"Helped him?" Theo asked. "How?"

"With ventriloquism," Emily whispered.

Theo felt the room tilt. His stool seemed to lift off the floor, and he grabbed hold of the counter to stop from tumbling backward. "You mean..."

"Those voices you heard. When you were watching Wendel Whispers practice. I was mimicking all of you. Throwing *my* voice."

"I taught her well," Mick said sadly.

"I'm so sorry, Theo. That was why you ran into me on the way back down the hill from the resort. I hadn't just come up from town. I was heading home after the ventriloquist's rehearsal."

"I asked her to do it," said Mick. "You can be mad at me."

But Emily agreed! Theo thought. *She could have said no!*

"And then at the balloon festival," Emily went on. "I threw my voice again, trying to spark an argument between Carter and Ridley." She twisted her lips and then demonstrated. *"Quit your yammering."*

She sounded just like Carter. And she had made it seem like it was coming from Mick's direction.

"Why would you do this?" Theo managed to ask. "Why try to make us fight? To break us apart?"

Mick squared himself to Theo, looking him straight in the face. "You might not have noticed," he began, "but over the past couple months, you kids have drawn quite a bit of attention. Getting involved with that jewel heist. Stopping Bosso's scheme. Interrupting Sandra's plans. I'm worried that you've drawn the attention of Kalagan, and he's not pleased."

"We have," said Theo. "The proof is on the poster."

"Indeed. By fighting back against his henchmen, you've made yourselves targets of Kalagan. Emily and I decided that the best way for you to escape his attention was to end your friendship."

Emily cleared her throat. "We needed to make you argue. Turn on each other. It didn't take much. And then you'd break up and stop being a thorn in Kalagan's side."

The whole situation suddenly came hurtling down onto Theo's shoulders. He slumped. This girl, his new friend, his first crush, had been lying to him ever since they had first met.

Theo looked at Mick. "Wait a moment. Why should I believe you? Breaking up the Misfits is what Kalagan wants, too. You could be working for him."

Mick shook his head sadly. "I already told you. I want nothing to do with Kalagan. Or Bosso. Or Sandra. Or even poor Dante. After everything we went through as children, I decided to leave magic behind." He paused, as if contemplating how much more to say. "It's not that I don't remember our meetings fondly. But after I saw what Kalagan was trying to do with magic, after what happened when he and Dante went head-to-head, I knew I had to distance myself from my former friends." He touched his neck, and Theo remembered his scar.

"What happened?" Theo asked. "What did Kalagan do to Mr. Vernon? Does it have something to do with the fire at the resort? The one that destroyed the rear wing?"

Watching the way Mick's eyelids closed briefly, Theo knew he had hit the nail on the head.

"It's not as simple as that," Mick said. "And I'm not sure that it's my tale to share. All I know is that Emily and I wanted to protect you. All of you."

Emily sniffed. "And we're telling you now so you will decide to end the bond between the Magic Misfits. If Dad and I were able to crack your solid foundation, think about what would happen if Kalagan were to try to infiltrate your circle."

"We know his following has grown," Mick continued. "You've met some of the cronies who work for him. He might actually be here in Mineral Wells. And if that's the case...please, Theo, consider what we're telling you."

"I do not believe I can listen to any more of this," Theo said, rising and stumbling to the door.

"You don't need to make a decision now," Emily called after him sadly. "But in time, I hope you'll realize we're right."

✳ ✳ ✳

As Theo stumbled home from the music shop, he half hoped to hear Emily's footsteps racing up behind him, tears streaming down her cheeks. *Forgive me, Theo!* But when he looked back, the sidewalk was empty, and he was alone.

Swinging open the front door of his house, Theo was greeted by his siblings, who were about to leave for another afternoon hike. "Come with us!" said Leo. "We're going to have a little music session in the woods."

How could Theo say no? He was happy to get lost in his violin for as long as he could.

By the time the family had reached the far side of the pond, Fiona said, "Oh, by the way! We signed up for that talent show tomorrow. You're going to join us, Theo, aren't you?"

It surprised Theo how quickly he came to a decision: "Yes. Yes, I will."

TWENTY

The next morning started out unusually hot and only got worse from there.

Leila answered the shop's door when Theo knocked.

"*Hellooooo*," Presto squawked from her perch.

Carter waved from the back of the shop, where he was entertaining Change-O by making a small red ball appear and disappear from his palm. The monkey screeched and slapped at Carter's hands.

It was the first time Theo had been back here in several days, and instead of the happiness the shop usually brought him, right now all he felt was dread.

He heard the bell chime as the door opened again behind him, and Ridley came in. When she saw Theo, her face turned pink beneath her freckles. But all she said was "The twins are on their way. Is everyone ready for tonight?"

"Can't wait!" said Leila, almost too enthusiastically.

"More than ready," Carter answered.

Change-O took one look at Ridley, hissed, and then dashed out of sight as Ridley hissed back. "Where's my Top Hat?" she asked.

Leila lifted one of the shop's top hats off a nearby table and revealed Ridley's pet rabbit sitting underneath. The creature greeted them, as usual, by scrunching up his nose.

Feeling a sudden need to smooth things over, Theo raised his bow over the rabbit. Top Hat floated off the table and landed in Ridley's lap. She snuggled the creature to her chest. "Thanks, Theo," she said quietly.

Somewhere, a clock went *tick, tock, tick, tock, tick, tock*.

From the balcony, there came a deafening crash. Everyone shrieked and then looked up to find the Golden twins peering down at them from the railing, wearing wide smiles. Izzy held a giant pair of metal cymbals. "I thought I'd take up a new hobby," she said. "I'm getting pretty good."

"Don't scare us like that!" Ridley scolded.

"How did you get in here?" asked Leila.

Olly pointed toward the entry to the Vernons' apartment. "Didn't you leave the side door open for us?"

Leila bit her lip. "Poppa must have forgotten to lock it when he left for work this morning."

"I'll take care of it," said Carter, grabbing the trick sword from behind the counter. Holding it up, he added, "Can't be too careful."

You do not know the half of it, Theo thought. Izzy descended the staircase, her brother following on her heels, but Theo waited patiently for Carter to return as the others buzzed about Wendel Whispers and his canceled show.

"Last night, Mr. Arnold looked like he might blow a gasket," said Olly.

"Mom and Dad said he was going to have to give all the ticket-holders refunds," said Izzy.

"I sure hope he doesn't find out it was our fault that the ventriloquist left town," said Olly. "He might make us tap-dance without our tap shoes!"

"Ouch!" said Izzy. "That would be worse than the time he made us do ballet wearing gorilla costumes!"

"That...didn't happen," Ridley guessed.

"But wouldn't it have been neat if it had?"

"But it *wasn't* our fault that Wendel left," Leila interrupted. "Someone at the resort put that code in the poster and wanted us to confront him. To show him the radio transmitters inside the doll heads. Someone wanted us to learn it wasn't him. They want us to be frightened."

That is only half-true, Theo thought. *Someone at the resort, yes. But also, someone right here in town. Mick Meridian. And Emily.* He wondered what would happen if he spoke these thoughts aloud.

"All clear!" Carter called from up above. He came down the steps and carefully placed the sword back inside the display case. "Don't tell your dads I took that, okay?" he said to Leila, and she pretended to zip her lips.

"Right!" said Ridley, petting Top Hat softly. "Now that we're all here, I'd like to call this meeting of the Magic Misfits to order."

Since the shop was closed and the lights were mostly

off, the group stayed near the counter, leaving their secret room behind the bookcase for another day.

Theo let them go on for a bit, but when they started to discuss a final rehearsal for the talent show that evening, he stood up and raised his hand. "May I please say something?" he asked, his voice on the verge of breaking.

His friends looked at him as if he had just announced that he was slowly turning into an iguana. (Which, I imagine, would have been preferable to what he was actually about to say.) "I...I am not going to perform with you tonight."

There was a quiet moment while this information sank in, before Theo's friends all looked like he had just stabbed them in the chests with the great fake sword in the glass case.

"What?" Ridley exclaimed, practically tossing Top Hat off her lap. *"Why not?"*

Theo wanted to say, *Because Kalagan has been watching us. He is mad that we have been interfering in his schemes, and if we go on like this, I fear that one, or all, of us will get hurt.* He wanted to say, *I know this because Mick and Emily revealed everything to me yesterday. They were trying to get us to fight with each other. This is for the best.*

Mostly he wanted to say, *You are my friends, and I am sorry.*

Instead, he answered, "My brothers and sisters need me to play my violin with them."

"That's ridiculous," said Ridley. "You're a *Magic Misfit*."

"Am I not allowed to be something else some-times?"

Ridley opened her mouth, obviously about to shout *no*, but Leila held her hand between them. "Theo, why can't you just do both?"

"I checked the rules," he answered. "Participants are only allowed to perform once."

"But we've already incorporated you into *our* routines," said Ridley, taking a different tack. "Even if you're not *performing*-performing, we'll still need your help."

She was right, but that was the point, was it not? To show that the Misfits could fall apart. To prove to Kalagan that he had nothing to worry about. That the Misfits were not heroes after all, but only a bunch of kids.

"I get it," said Carter with a sad smile. "You don't want to disappoint your family."

"I am so sorry," Theo answered finally. "But it is not only about my family." He needed to drive in the stake. He knew that Mick and Emily had been right, in their own twisted way. He needed to finish this. "We have been fighting too much. I think...I think I need to take a break."

"Breaks are good," said Izzy. "We always take breaks between our performances."

"I was thinking about a longer break," Theo clarified. "My brother told me a while ago that I have been neglecting my violin. I am beginning to agree."

No one spoke. *Tick, tock, tick, tock, tick, tock.*

There were tears in Ridley's eyes. And since they were accompanied by the further flushing of her cheeks, Theo could not tell if they were tears of sadness or of rage. He looked to the others. They gaped at him in shock—everyone except for Olly, who was staring at the front door.

"When did Mr. Vernon get home?" he asked.

Carter shook his head. "We haven't heard from Mr. Vernon since—" He stopped when he noticed the figure standing in the shadowed vestibule just outside. This person was tall, made even taller by the top hat perched on his head. A long black cloak draped from his shoulders, flapping slightly in the breeze—a bit of its red silk lining winking at them. A cloud of smoke swirled, and a flicker of orange glowed from the end of a cigarette.

"*Dad?*" Leila asked, heading for the door.

"Leila, *shh!*" Theo whispered. "When have we ever seen Mr. Vernon *smoking*?"

Leila froze, her hand almost on the knob.

"But then...who?" Carter whispered back.

The Misfits stood in stunned silence, their own personal dramas suddenly shrinking down into nothing.

"Whoever that is, he's been listening to us," Ridley said in a hush. She glanced around the group in disbelief. She gulped. "Do you think he might be—"

The figure took off then, racing away from the vestibule and into the street. A car honked as it barely missed hitting him. He dashed across the lawn and headed around the corner near the barbershop.

"What are we waiting for?" Ridley asked, pushing toward the door and swinging it open. "After him!"

"It's not safe!" said Carter. "We should call someone."

"He's getting away!" said Leila, rushing after Ridley.

Already, the two were outside at the curb.

Theo took off after them, leaving the twins behind with Carter.

It did not take long to make it across the town green to the barbershop corner. Theo rushed by Ridley and Leila and raced around the bend, then he skidded to a halt in the middle of the sidewalk, his heart creeping into his throat.

A few feet ahead, the figure in the top hat and cape seemed to be hovering just over the ground. But there was something strange about the man's appearance now. Theo could not see his neck. And there was a stick of a shadow where the feet should have been.

For almost five seconds, the figure did not move.

"You there!" Theo called out and then stepped forward. Leila came from behind and clutched at his arm, but Theo went on. "Who are you?"

The figure did not answer. The breeze fluttered the hem of the cape.

Ridley and Leila followed Theo as he approached the floating figure, terrified. But before he could get close, the cape slid slowly off a coat hanger and then dropped to the bluestone sidewalk below. Theo let out a ragged breath. The hat was perched atop a wooden coatrack. There was no floating figure. Someone had placed the rack for them to find.

This had been a disappearing act.

Theo spun, looking for anyone who might have been watching them. He caught a whiff of smoke. Not far from the base of the strange coatrack were the remains of a cigarette that had been stomped out. Carefully, he picked it up. Small words printed on its filter caught his eye.

Good choice, Theo.

He held back a gasp and then pocketed the filter. He could not let the others see what he had found.

Carter and the twins appeared from around the corner.

Leila snatched the hat off the coatrack. "This is my father's," she said, holding it up and showing them the label. She bent down and picked up the cloak. "This too."

"Whoever did this must have taken them from our house," Carter answered.

"Why, though?" Leila asked.

Theo sighed, growing more certain about his talent show decision. "To let us know that he can."

The Misfits slowly returned to the magic shop with Mr. Vernon's items.

"That was really stupid of you guys not to follow us immediately," said Ridley to Carter and the twins. "We need to stick together."

The word *stupid* smacked Theo's forehead like a stray mechanical dragonfly. "Do not talk to them like that," he heard himself say. "Just because you are scared does not give you the right to be mean."

Ridley's face turned fuchsia. She puffed out her cheeks. "You're a...a *jerk*, Theo Stein-Meyer!" she shouted. "I'm not sad that you're quitting the Magic Misfits. I'm happy!"

"Well, I feel that *you* have not been particularly friendly these last few weeks, Ridley Larsen. And I am not quitting," Theo scrambled to answer. "I am merely performing with—"

"We know exactly what you're doing," Ridley said. She faced the others. "Listen, I'll see you guys here tonight before the show." Looking at Theo, she added, "I don't care if I ever see *you* again." Then she barreled through the doorway of the magic shop and out onto the sidewalk.

Theo sighed. Leila squeezed his shoulder. "She didn't mean that."

"I think she did, actually," he answered. His head felt hollow. "All this is for the best. See you tonight. I will be cheering the Misfits on."

He left them and did not look back.

Instead of going home to meet up with his siblings, Theo turned toward the music shop. The closer he got, the angrier he felt. By the time he reached the entrance, he was so upset that his hands were actually shaking.

He found Emily just inside. "That was not okay," he said to her, trying to keep his voice low.

"I don't know what you mean," she said, shaking her head. Theo held out the cigarette butt for her to see. She scowled. "What am I looking at?"

"A message from your father," he answered as evenly as he could.

Her blue eyes seemed to pale as she read the words

printed on it. *Good choice, Theo.* "My father doesn't smoke."

"That is not the point," Theo said. "He wanted to let me know he is happy that I decided not to perform with the Magic Misfits tonight." He shared the story of the figure in the vestibule of the magic shop. And the chase. And the coatrack in the middle of the sidewalk. "He was listening to us."

Emily shook her head. "My father's been working in his office all morning."

Theo remembered the feeling of the afternoon he had first met her—how he had been drawn to her by an invisible thread. He thought of the connection he had felt while walking back down from the resort with her. Of the dreams of them flying high over Mineral Wells. "How can I believe you?" he asked.

Emily frowned. "He's back there now. You can ask him yourself."

"But how can I believe him?"

She sighed. "Look, Theo, I know we deceived you."

"That is just another way of saying *We lied.*"

"Call it what you want. But I followed my father's instructions because I knew it was the right thing to do. To keep you guys safe. To keep the town safe. It was a hard decision because...I like you, Theo. I really do. And I didn't mean to hurt you. Or your friends. I hope someday you all can find a way to forgive me."

"I did not tell the others about what you did. They do not know they have anything to forgive."

Emily nodded at the cigarette remains in his palm. "The message was right," she answered, "no matter who delivered it. You made a *good choice*, Theo. Kalagan will stop seeing you as a threat. He'll leave you alone now."

"I hope you are correct," Theo said quietly. "For all our sakes."

TWENTY-ONE

At seven o'clock, Theo left his house with his brothers and sisters. Carrying their instruments, they made their way to the town green, where they found a large crowd gathering for the talent show.

Picnic blankets were spread out, covering the grass like a patchwork quilt. Some people had brought folding chairs. There was a buzz in the air as the townspeople passed around the printed lists of performers and placed bets on who was the favorite to win the competition. *The Magic Misfits* were on everyone's lips, and Theo felt a pain in his chest knowing that he would not be a part of their group tonight. Looking toward Vernon's Magic Shop, he watched his friends through the window as they fixed one another's costumes and readied themselves to come outside and cross the street.

He clenched his teeth and mentally told himself to *Buck up, Theo*. This was not forever. It was only until they caught Kalagan and stopped him from tormenting the town of Mineral Wells. And yet, how would they stop him if they could not work together?

It felt like a mystery with no solution.

Leo waved Theo over to where the list of performers was posted at the back of the gazebo. "We're up first," he said. "Are you ready, little brother?" Theo pressed his lips together and nodded. He feared that if he spoke, his voice would crack, and his eyes would tear up. He clutched the handle of his violin case and then felt for the folded bow in his pants pocket—the one that could do magic, make things float and fly, make people smile and gasp and clap. But then he remembered he had left that one at home. Tonight, he only needed the bow that could play music.

A few minutes later, Mayor McFadden, dressed in a sharply cut blue-checked suit, took the stage, shifting his feet in front of the microphone stand. "Hello,

Mineral Wells! Welcome to the Thirty-Third Annual Talent Show and Competition!" The crowd whooped and hollered, proud of their little town. "The talent here this evening is sure to knock your socks off. Now sit back, relax, and let's give a nice round of applause for our first act." He glanced at a small piece of paper in his palm, then announced: "The Stein-Meyer Family Band!"

In the gazebo, Fiona stood in the center and the rest of the siblings formed a half circle around her. She motioned for Theo to play an A. The others tuned their instruments. A hush fell over the crowd. The sky was darkening, and the streetlights began to glow.

Theo glanced again at the magic shop, but the lights were now dim. As he prepared to play, he told himself that it was for the best. He followed Fiona's lead, drawing his bow across the strings, making them sing and hum, causing the air itself to vibrate and dance. His brothers and other sister joined in, and before long, the audience was clapping in time, just like the metronome Mick Meridian had gifted him.

When the Stein-Meyers were finished, the crowd applauded generously. So generously that Theo wondered if he and his siblings had not already sealed the win. They left the stage excitedly and gathered on the large blanket that Mr. and Mrs. Stein-Meyer had earlier placed in the center of the lawn.

Other acts performed well, but people seated nearby continually whispered to Theo that he and his family had done better. One thing that stuck out to him was the number of Darling Daniels he saw in the crowd. None of these people knew yet that each of the dolls contained a radio transmitter broadcasting their conversations to a hidden receiver. What would they do when the *Gazette* printed the truth?

Eventually, the mayor approached the microphone again and announced the act that Theo was dreading. "I would like to welcome some recent local heroes, the self-proclaimed *Magic Misfits*! I wonder what they're going to save us from this evening." He chuckled.

The crowd laughed and then applauded loudly as five kids took the stage. Theo, the missing sixth, slumped down, hoping none of them would look out and see him with his family.

His friends were dressed in their finest. Carter had on a black suit with tails and a shiny top hat. Leila wore sparkly black pants and a loosened straitjacket. Ridley looked smashing in an emerald-green number embellished with glittering fringe. And the twins wore matching plaid rompers, straw boat hats, leather wing tips, and black socks pulled up over their knees. Most impressive, however, was what the animal assistants were wearing. Top Hat was dressed in a tiny black top hat strapped between his ears. He sat in Ridley's lap. Hanging from Presto's feathered neck was a sparkly pendant that looked like a replica of the Star of Africa, the diamond that Bosso had attempted to steal.

She perched on Leila's shoulder. Change-O had on a bright red bow tie that was attached to his harness and leash, which Carter clutched tightly.

Ridley took the microphone from the mayor and waved to the crowd. "We're so happy to be here, friends!" she called out. "We plan on continuing to perform for the people of Mineral Wells for years to come!"

Theo's skin crawled. He was unsure whether she had meant to hurl that statement at him...or at Kalagan. He looked around again, certain that the mesmerist was hiding among the townspeople. But he observed only the smiling faces of the audience, anticipating magical delights from the young performers on stage.

To Theo's horror, their act faltered from the very start. During a simple card-toss trick, Carter managed to drop several from the deck. He flushed red, apologized quietly, then went on, pretending to offer Change-O the next choice of cards. But then Change-O attempted to run off stage, and Carter nearly tripped trying to catch him. Ridley wheeled her chair over the monkey's leash, and he screeched and scowled.

Theo thought back to their rehearsals—*he* was supposed to have handed the pack to Carter from his pocket. Could this mistake have been Theo's fault?

The audience laughed anyway, thankfully thinking that it was all part of the fun. Next, Ridley held up Top Hat to show the crowd. The twins raised a large cloth in front of the rabbit, but they whipped it away before Ridley could switch out his top hat for a tiny Easter bonnet. Both hats fell off Ridley's lap. The rabbit leapt down, and Leila had to scoop everything up and return it all to Ridley, who was so embarrassed she did not bother trying the trick again.

This time, it was obvious that a mistake had been made, and the audience began to murmur. Again, this had been a trick that Theo was meant to be a part of, and he was certain that the twins' error was because he had left them in the lurch.

"They're not very good, are they?" Gio whispered to Cleo.

Theo refrained from telling them it was because he had chosen his family over his friends. "We are usually much better," he said. "There was not much time to practice."

The twins managed to get through a comedic routine with their pet mice with no mess-ups, but it did little to win over the crowd again.

People were beginning to look bored. Near the far

side of the park, a group began to boo. Theo glanced over and saw the boys who had bullied them a few weeks prior. The one who had thrown mud at him, Tyler, was the loudest.

Then he saw Emily run over, hands on her hips. Tyler and his cronies sat back down again.

Theo needed to do something too. The Magic Misfits did not deserve this ridicule. He felt himself stand up, his violin and bow in hand. Leo called out, "Where are you going, little brother?" But Theo simply stepped around the couple sitting in front of him and made his way to the stage.

His friends glanced down at him as he climbed the steps. "What are you doing here?" Ridley snapped. "You can't perform twice."

He recalled what Mr. Vernon had told them. "I'm being your *out*. Let me help with the finale." He looked for Emily on the edge of the crowd. Catching his gaze, she shook her head. But he did not care. He never should have left the Misfits.

"We'll be disqualified, Theo," said Leila.

"Who cares?" Carter answered. "We're not going to win at this point anyway."

Ridley sighed and looked to the twins. They both nodded enthusiastically. "Fine," she said. "But this doesn't mean you're forgiven."

Theo smiled happily. "I understand." He listened for the cooing noise he knew should be coming from the gazebo's roof.

You see, Theo had let his doves loose just before leaving home that evening. Then, during his walk to the park with his siblings, he had signaled for the birds to follow, just in case he needed them. Neither the audience nor the Misfits had noticed.

Leila came to the front of the stage. "Ladies and gentlemen, I'd like to introduce a special guest who will be assisting me with the final segment of our performance this evening. Meet Theo Stein-Meyer!"

Over a smattering of applause, one of the judges called out, "If he participates, young lady, none of you will be eligible for the grand prize."

"It doesn't matter," said Carter.

"Theo is an indispensable member of our group," Leila added.

The twins gave Theo high fives.

Ridley crossed her arms but nodded begrudgingly.

"Suit yourselves," said the judge, sitting back down.

The Misfits conferred. Theo told them his plan. "Leila, go ahead with what we practiced," he said. "But then follow my lead. The finale will blow them away."

He stepped back and rested his bow against the strings. He moved his hand briskly, and a jolt echoed across the town green. The audience quieted and watched the magicians skeptically.

"Good people of Mineral Wells!" Leila called out. "If I may beg your attention! We have a tale to tell you! A reenactment of the scene from several weeks ago, when a group of gangsters broke into my father's magic shop and tried to hold us hostage!"

A murmuring rose up from the crowd. After all the rumors that had been floating around, people were excited to hear the story straight from the source.

Leila went on, embellishing the events just the way the Misfits had practiced. Theo accompanied her with his violin, playing a dramatic riff when Carter, Ridley, Olly, and Izzy—creeping around the stage like cartoonish bad guys—pretended to be the frown clowns. His violin let out a triumphant squeal when Leila captured the villains with a long white rope and tied them up. The four formed a line across the gazebo, arms raised in front of themselves, wrists exposed.

"The Magic Misfits need a volunteer to check that these bindings are solid," she called out. "Is anyone willing to help?"

Theo held on to a suspenseful trill as he scanned the audience. "Leila," he whispered. "Over there."

"You!" Leila shouted, pointing to Emily Meridian. "Please make your way to the stage."

Moments later, she was climbing the stairs. Emily's eyes were worried as she leaned toward him and whispered, "This is a terrible mistake."

"I am sorry you feel that way," Theo said simply.

"Miss, would you mind checking that the knots are tight?" asked Leila, directing her voice out at the audience.

Emily did as she was told. Through thin lips, she called, "Plenty tight. Almost too tight, Leila."

Leila blinked, a bit flustered. "Thank you....You may step down."

Once Emily had put enough distance between herself and the group, Leila winked at Theo. It was the signal they had agreed upon at their last rehearsal.

She clapped and the knots were undone. She whipped the rope away.

The next part happened quickly, while the crowd was still *ooohing* and *aaahing*.

Theo placed his violin and bow gently on the gazebo floor. He looked intensely at Carter, Ridley, Olly, and Izzy to let them know that he was about to make his move. Then he called out to his doves in the way that only he knew, blowing quickly through his teeth. Six white birds fluttered down from the roof of the gazebo and landed on the Misfits—one on each of their heads or hats, which they struggled to keep steady.

The audience gasped, then broke into applause. Finally, things were going right. Did it matter that they would be disqualified? Was this not the most important part of the performance—*creating wonder*?

Theo did not have his magic bow in his pocket, so he raised his arms instead. Keeping his palms facing downward, Theo spread his fingers and then began to lift his hands upward. The birds on the Misfits' heads and flapped their wings. Each of the kids suddenly appeared to rise from the gazebo floor, as if the birds were carrying them. Up and up they went. Higher. Higher. One inch, two, three, four, *five*!

Several members of the audience stood in surprise. Some seemed to cry out in fear. Carter wore a look of delight. Leila clutched her fists to her chin. The twins giggled. Ridley smirked. And Theo kept a focused expression plastered on his face, as if it were taking all his might to control the birds and the levitation of his friends.

He knew he did not have much time before someone came around the side of the stage and discovered the secret of his illusion, so he whistled loudly and the birds left the heads of the Misfits, flying out over the crowd and circling the town green.

The Magic Misfits continued to float above the floor for several seconds, until Theo lowered his hands, smoothly but quickly, and each of them settled back onto firm footing.

The audience practically exploded. They leapt to their feet, cheering—even Tyler and the other bullies, Theo noticed. The Misfits came to the front of the stage, barely able to contain their excitement. They grasped hands and raised them up, and together, they took a long, well-earned bow.

— TWENTY-TWO —

They did not win, of course.

That honor went to Miss Carmen Halprin and her trio of dancing dachshunds—Henny, Penny, and Bruce. The judges handed her the trophy and the award money, which she accepted to the din of polite applause.

Everyone knew which of the acts had had a real impact, if only at its end.

Meeting up with the other Misfits off stage, Theo found that Ridley was true to her word, and not yet ready to be forgiving. "So, you ruin the day, and when you rush in at the last minute, you expect to be hailed as a hero?"

"Oh, leave him alone, Ridley," said Leila, throwing her arms around Theo. "We've all been through a lot this week."

"Every week, it seems," Carter added.

Izzy smiled. "Hopefully we can keep the villains at bay every *other* week from now on."

"Hey," said Olly, pointing to the other end of the lawn. "Isn't that Mr. Meridian and Emily waving to us?"

"Let's go say hi," Leila said, and started to cross the lawn. "I want to thank Emily for her help." Carter, Ridley, and the twins followed.

Theo thought of what Emily had said to him on stage: *This is a terrible mistake.* Was she going to tell the Misfits the truth? He thought about asking his friends to stay put, but he knew that would only make them ask why. "Wait," he said, but no one heard him.

Crossing the town green after his friends, Theo was stopped by familiar voices calling to him.

To his great relief, his family greeted him with hugs and congratulations, despite the fact that rescuing his friends from embarrassment had caused the Stein-Meyer Family Band to lose their chance at local fame and glory as well. "I'm proud of you, little brother," Leo said, rubbing his head. Then he leaned close. "But make sure you keep practicing that violin. You're quite gifted."

"I will. I promise." He glanced toward the other end of the lawn, where Mick Meridian appeared already to be in deep conversation with the Magic Misfits. "Could you please hold on to my violin case for a moment? I shall return shortly."

By the time he reached the others, he could sense something was off. Carter was clutching Change-O's leash so tightly his knuckles were white. Leila's jaw was dropped in shock, and Presto mimicked her, perched on her shoulder. Olly and Izzy looked like someone had just insulted their matching rompers. And Ridley's face had turned a reddish color that managed to erase the freckles from her cheeks entirely.

Even though he knew what would happen when he opened his mouth, Theo still had to ask, "What is wrong?" They turned to him as if he had appeared out of nowhere.

Emily said, "We had to tell them, Theo."

"Tell them what?" he asked, his voice barely audible.

"That *I* was the ventriloquist from the Emerald Ring," answered Mick.

"Oh?" Theo said vaguely. "Wow."

"And about what Emily and I have been doing to all of you."

"Throwing my voice," said Emily. "Trying to save you by keeping you apart."

For the first time, Theo thought she sounded like someone who had been brainwashed. As if her father had filled her head with conspiratorial nonsense.

Then, to Theo's utter horror, Emily turned to the Misfits and said, "Theo knew. My father and I told him all this yesterday."

His friends turned to him, and he felt himself stop breathing at their looks of shock and anger.

"Is that true?" Carter asked.

"I—I—" It was all he could manage to say.

"That answers your question, Carter," Ridley murmured, glaring at Theo.

"Now, hold on," said Leila. "We have to hear Theo's side of the story." She sounded unsure.

Theo composed himself. "They *did* tell me yesterday what they had done. Throwing voices and trying to make us fight. But they also explained to me *why* they did it." He glanced at Emily, who avoided his eyes. "They were worried that Kalagan would target us," he said. "They believed that the only way to remove his bull's-eye was for us to stop being friends."

"*That's* why you wouldn't perform with us? You listened to them?" Ridley asked. "That's horrible, Theo."

"When I made the decision, I was worried that they were right. I did it so that none of us would get hurt the way that Mr. Meridian was hurt in the fire at the resort."

"How on Earth did you know my scar was from the fire, Theo?" Mick said.

"I did not," Theo replied. "But thank you for confirming it."

Mick grimaced, but nodded. Theo felt a slight thrill at having turned the tables on Mick and Emily, even in this small way.

"There's so much more that we need to share with you," Mick finally said. "In time, you'll know the truth. But for now, we think you all are in great danger. I know Kalagan. But I also know Dante Vernon."

"My dad is the best," said Leila with a scoff.

"He's prideful and he's reckless. He thinks of himself as invincible."

"Invisible?" said Olly.

"But that's only sometimes!" Izzy added.

"*Invincible*," Mick repeated. "As though nothing and no one can hurt him. Why else would he continue to ask the six of you to put yourselves in harm's way just to help him settle his differences?"

The Misfits had no answer for this. Theo thought of what Mr. Vernon had done in just the last few months. Suggesting they dress up in costumes and break into Bosso's hotel room. Hiding truths about Sandra Santos. Thinking that protecting his ledger from those who wished to steal it was more important than keeping his own daughter safe. And most recently, leaving them to fend for themselves, knowing there was a chance Kalagan would come after them.

Mick sighed. "Let me tell you a story."

✴ ✴ ✴

According to Mick, the current Emerald Ring numbers were too many to count.

However, it had begun with only two: Dante and Lyle. They wished to hold magic aloft as an ideal entertainment. It was how they created a sense of wonder in their own world.

Kalagan, however, had tried to get the group to see that their skills had the potential to make money. He had picked up several books about psychology and hypnotism. Mesmerism. He practiced on the members of the Emerald Ring.

And then everything turned on its head one summer, shortly after the sign-up list for the Mineral Wells talent show was posted. The Emerald Ring was the clear favorite to win. Yet the group could not agree on which of their skills should conclude the act.

Dante thought he could come up with a way to make every member of the Emerald Ring disappear at once.

Kalagan wanted to mesmerize several members of the audience into placing their wallets and jewelry into a velvet sack and then make them set it on fire. The sack would burn just as the volunteers realized what they had done. But the final reveal would have Kalagan removing his top hat, showing the victims that their belongings were safe, balanced perfectly on his head.

Dante did not trust that Kalagan would return the belongings safely or soundly.

The argument grew heated until Sandra suggested that the Emerald Ring hold their own contest: Dante's routine versus Kalagan's act.

The boys agreed to meet in the basement of the lodge at the resort, where Bobby, Sandra, Mick, and Lyle had set up a platform the size and shape of the gazebo floor.

Dante performed first, issuing a request for several members of the Ring to stand on the makeshift stage as if for a curtain call. Surrounded by stacks of boxes, swirls of dust, and curtains of cobwebs, he showed them what to do to create his illusion. It worked flawlessly, and Dante bowed deeply, his friends applauding.

Then it was Kalagan's turn. He asked each member of the Emerald Ring to give him their most valuable possessions, and he put them all inside his velvet bag. He made a long candlestick appear out of nowhere, then snapped his fingers, the wick bursting alight.

It is difficult to say exactly what happened next.

Some of the kids said it was an accident.

Others were certain that it was done on purpose.

Regardless, the fire spread quickly, moving from the makeshift stage to the stacks of dusty boxes. After that, flames leapt to the ceiling and devoured the wooden joists that held up the floor overhead.

Sandra and Lyle and Dante were able to escape the basement through a secret door into the bootlegging tunnels. Bobby, Mick, and Kalagan managed to make it up the stairs to the first-floor hallway. Once there, they encountered chaos. Guests were rushing about, trying to escape as the fire and smoke overwhelmed them. Kalagan split off from the other boys, running up another flight of stairs, shouting that he needed to find his parents.

Bolting toward one of the windows, Mick tripped. A burning piece of the ceiling fell. It trapped him as flames crawled up his back toward his neck. Then there was darkness.

Bobby had thrown a blanket over his friend, putting out the blaze. The two boys limped out into the night, pain flaring across Mick's damaged skin.

The lodge burned for hours, even as the Mineral Wells Fire Department put up a valiant fight to extinguish it. By dawn, much of the structure still stood, but it had been charred beyond recognition.

So had the young magicians' friendship.

★ ★ ★

Quiet lingered among the Misfits. They glanced at one another for several seconds until Theo finally asked the obvious: "What happened next?"

"I spent months in the hospital, recovering from my wounds. I had several surgeries and grafts, and I basically had to learn how to move again." Mick paused. "Kalagan managed to get out of the burning building...but his parents, who worked there and were trying to help the guests, did not. He was sent to an orphanage. He kept sneaking out to come back to Mineral Wells, though. He and Bobby remained close, but Kalagan blamed Dante and Lyle for what had happened. For escaping and leaving us alone in the basement. He never forgave them."

"And you?" Theo asked. "Did you blame Mr. Vernon for leaving?"

Mick sighed. "I don't believe what happened was an accident. He played a part. Afterward, I wanted nothing more to do with magic or performing. The members of the Ring all grew up and moved on. Or so I thought. Kalagan has let his anger transform him. I would suspect that Dante Vernon allowed his own guilt to do the same. He's spent years trying to correct his mistakes...and now it appears he's trying to do it through the six of you."

"Mr. Vernon has a lot of faith in us," Theo said, trying hard to believe it.

Leila nodded, wiping tears from her cheeks. "My dad loves us with all his heart."

Mick turned to Theo. "Joining your friends on stage this evening undid everything we've accomplished in the past couple weeks, Theo. Kalagan's spies are watching. And now they know that your group is as strong as ever."

"Maybe that is a good thing, Mr. Meridian," said Theo. "We cannot fight back unless we *are* strong. Emily knows that better than anyone else. She is the one who took down Tyler when he threatened us during rehearsal."

"But she fought Tyler alone," said Mick. "And she has trained and practiced and gotten better, *alone*. I suggest you all do the same."

"We're the Magic Misfits," said Ridley, clutching Top Hat in her lap. "We do magic. *That's* what we practice. And it can be just as powerful as fists."

"But Kalagan knows this. He will only use it against you. You *and* Vernon."

And again silence.

Tick, tock, tick, tock, tick, tock went the clock on the wall.

Theo finally managed to catch Emily's eye. "I thought we were friends," he said quietly.

She returned his gaze. "I thought you would under-stand," she said with no emotion.

Tick, tock, tick, tock, tick, tock went Theo's heartbeat, keeping time to a music that was no longer playing.

As he turned away, the ground suddenly shook underneath him. Half a second later, a blast sounded. It was so loud that the last members of the crowd remaining on the town green covered their ears instinctively.

Theo watched as the great glass windows at the front of the magic shop exploded outward.

TWENTY-THREE

Pieces of the stone facade littered the sidewalk and the street. The crowd ran for cover as the Misfits watched the building implode. There came a great cracking sound as the slate roof caved in, and the front of the building leaned precariously backward into a crater where the floor of the shop had been moments earlier.

"The bootlegging tunnels," Leila said breathlessly. "The one beneath the shop must have collapsed!"

"You think this was an accident?" Carter shouted.

"I don't know! Stop yelling at me!"

"Kalagan," Ridley declared. "He knows those tunnels run through the town!"

Theo swallowed hard, then glanced at Mick and Emily, who looked as horrified as the rest of them. Then he remembered the anagram from the Grand Oak's poster for Wendel Whispers's show.

"*Magic Misfits crumble*," he whispered. He thought of the cigarette butt he had found earlier that day. The writing on the filter had read: *Good choice, Theo*. He was not supposed to have performed with the Misfits. He turned to his friends. "The poster *was* a warning. We did not listen." He needed to see the shop. "Stay with the animals," he called back to Ridley.

As Theo ran into the street, he heard footsteps behind him. Soon Carter and Leila had joined him. "Poppa," Leila whimpered. "He's supposed to be at work. I need to call him."

Stopping at the curb, Theo could see into the building through a cloud of dissipating dust. "I do not believe your telephone exists anymore."

Sirens rose in the distance. The Mineral Wells Fire Department was on its way.

"What do we do?" asked Carter.

Theo looked around for his family. But he couldn't

make out any faces from the crowd. Everyone had moved to the safety of the far side of the park.

"Hey, you kids," a voice said from nearby. "It's not safe here."

Standing in the entry of the shop next door stood a figure dressed all in black. With growing fear, Theo understood that this was the same man who had been listening in on the Magic Misfits' meeting that morning, the same man who had run off and turned into a coatrack dressed in Mr. Vernon's clothing. Theo felt

Leila squeeze his left hand as Carter took his right. Together they backed away. "You hear me?" he called out again. "This is the last place you want to be."

With a black-gloved hand, the man reached inside his cape and withdrew a small black stick. Each end of it was marked white. It was a traditional magic wand, like the ones Mr. Vernon had displayed in a glass jar at the front of the store.

The store that was no more.

The man was moving the wand in such a way that Theo felt he could not tear away his gaze. Then, with a flick of his wrist, the man transformed the wand into something else.

Long and sharp, a blade glinted under the street-lights.

"Run!" Theo shouted to his friends.

They bolted around the corner.

The sky was black now, and starlight sprayed fully across the heavens. Theo raced with Carter and Leila as the street inclined. He nearly tripped over the cob-blestones but then found his footing and kept on.

The streetlights on this block had gone out with the blast. The trio ran past darkened storefronts. Footfalls echoed from behind them. The man was not far away.

Theo tried to not think about the sharp instrument he had seen in his clenched fist.

"Which way?" asked Leila, breathing heavily.

"Whichever way is *away*," Carter answered. "He's too close for us to lose him."

Theo grabbed their arms and yanked them into an alleyway that had appeared ahead.

Brick walls pressed in on them, and the slit of the alley's exit grew larger as their sprinting brought them closer. Looking over his shoulder, Theo saw movement at the alley's entrance. The blur of a shadow.

The three burst into a wide darkened parking lot. The backs of several stores and a few homes had created a secluded area. The electricity was still out. The silhouette of a church steeple rose up high overhead.

"This way." Theo pointed toward a stone path around the side of the church.

Racing footfalls echoed across the asphalt behind them. It did not seem to matter where they might hide. The figure was anticipating their next steps.

And he was only getting closer.

Carter reached into his pocket. He snapped his fingers, and a glint of fire lit the night. He hurled the flash paper back at the figure. It flew through the air like a falling star and landed at the man's feet. The figure jumped over the embers and continued his pursuit.

Leila wiggled her shoulders and slipped out of her straitjacket, her black shirt allowing her to blend into the night. Halfway down the path beside the church, she turned back and flung the jacket at the figure. The arms seemed to wrap around his face, as if they had minds of their own. For the first time, the man slowed—perhaps even stumbled.

Leila veered off the path, dragging the boys into a patch of forsythia bushes. She motioned for them to stay quiet. Crouching inside the brush, the three watched the man struggle with the straitjacket only a few feet away.

Within seconds, he whipped it off and threw it to the ground. He stooped to pick up his top hat. Finally, he noticed that the kids had disappeared. He stopped in the middle of the garden path, glancing in all directions.

Theo held his breath. Leila clutched his arm. Carter covered his mouth. Were Ridley and the twins okay? Theo wondered. What about Emily and Mick?

The figure fixed his gaze on the shrubbery. He

stepped onto the grass, only moments from discovering their hiding spot.

From around the corner of the church, Theo heard a voice whisper, "Let us split up. Carter goes that way. Leila takes the other. And I will circle around the other side." Goose bumps rose on the back of Theo's neck. It was his *own* voice!

Then he realized it had to be Emily. She was imitating him, throwing her voice to confuse their pursuer.

The man took the bait. He bolted back to the path and raced around the corner where the fake Theo had spoken.

Carter and Leila stared at Theo with eyes like moons. *Emily*, he mouthed. *Helping us.* He nodded toward the parking lot from where they had come. Carefully, they crept out of the forsythia and padded quietly through the grass, listening for the sound of footsteps. But none came.

They were nearly halfway across the parking lot, heading for the safety of the alley, when a singsong voice called out from behind them, *"I'm Darling Daniel. Who are you?"*

Turning back, they saw the dark figure standing

only a dozen or so feet away. Frozen in place. The world started to spin. Theo felt like he was part of a magic act that he had not volunteered for.

"Leave us alone!" called Leila.

"You don't want to mess with the Misfits!" shouted Carter.

"*I'm Darling Daniel,*" echoed the voice of Mr. Whispers's dummy. "*Who are you?*"

"We are the Magic Misfits!" Theo yelled so hard his throat hurt. "And you are going to pay for what you have done!"

A new voice came from the frozen figure. A familiar voice. "*I'm Dante Vernon,*" it said. "*What...have...I...done?*"

"Dad?" Leila asked.

"That is *not* your dad," Theo reassured her.

A spark flashed at the base of the man's cape. Flames erupted there, hurrying upward before engulfing the figure entirely. Theo, Leila, and Carter clung to one another in horror as they watched the man burn.

Laughter sounded off the buildings that enclosed the parking lot.

And Theo realized that it was only a trick. A misdirection. A bunch of clothes hanging from a coatrack.

Again. The longer the trio remained distracted by the spectacle of the blazing man, the more time the villain would have to set up the next illusion.

Whatever was coming could be deadly.

"Come on," he said, tugging at Carter's and Leila's sleeves. But when he turned, he smacked into something hard.

No, not something, Theo realized. *Someone.*

Looking up, he saw the black brim of a top hat blocking out the stars. "Kalagan!" Theo choked out.

Strong fingers closed around his arms.

"Gotcha," the man said, and began to chuckle.

— TWENTY-FOUR —

Leila and Carter screamed and ducked away.

Kalagan pulled Theo close, spinning him and hugging an arm across his chest. Something pressed into Theo's throat just beneath his chin.

"Wh-what do you want from us?" Theo stammered.

"I want you all to...disappear," said a low, scratchy voice, completely unlike the other voices they had already heard from him. "You've made a *bad choice, Theo*."

"Let him go," Carter pleaded. He held out his hands to show he had no tricks up his sleeves.

"Please," Leila added. "He's just a kid."

"*Just a kid*," Kalagan echoed. "You *kids* have already done immense damage this summer. My plans—"

From across the lot came a jumble of footsteps and the sound of spinning wheels. They stopped abruptly on the opposite side of the burning coatrack. "Theo!" Ridley screamed. Then her face darkened as she focused on the man in the top hat and cape. "You... you *villain*! If you hurt him, I'll...I'll..."

"You'll what?" asked Kalagan, amused, his throat filled with gravel. "You'll squirt me with water from your wheelchair?" He turned to Carter and Leila. "You'll slice me with your cards and then tie me up with dental floss?" He glanced past the blaze and called out to Olly and Izzy. "You'll tap-dance me into oblivion?" His laugh coughed from his throat like a steam engine gaining speed. "How very *cute*. You kids have no idea who you're dealing with."

A new voice came from behind Theo and Kalagan: "Neither do you."

Before Theo could think, he heard a wallop and a crack and a shriek that nearly burst his eardrums. He was pitched forward, the end of the wand-knife scraping his skin. He scrambled away from Kalagan, then turned to find Emily Meridian standing over him, her hands raised in a martial arts position.

Kalagan rolled out of reach, then scrambled to his feet, putting all his weight on only one leg. He winced in pain. "You've made the mistake of your life."

Theo whistled, loud and long, trying to distract Kalagan and call for help at the same time. Kalagan looked confused, but only for a moment, giving Emily time to motion for Theo, Carter, and Leila to join Ridley and the twins on the opposite side of the fire. "I doubt it," she told Kalagan. "These Misfits are stronger than you'll ever know."

He raised his wand and pointed it at her. "Stronger than your father, I hope." He touched his neck where Mick's scar would have been.

The comment caught Emily off guard. It was all the time he needed. He charged toward her, no longer limping, his blade glinting orange from the fire.

There was a fluttering overhead. Theo did not wait. He whistled the signal, and his doves dove down toward Kalagan. Their white wings flashed wickedly as their claws scratched at his face. He screamed and tried to duck away.

You see, my friend, Theo had taken Mr. Vernon's

advice to heart: *A magician must prepare for all possible outcomes.* In between music sessions with his siblings and spying on Wendel Whispers with his friends, Theo had been practicing this trick with his beloved doves. Ever since he had tried a version of it on the bully Tyler some weeks ago, he'd known he needed to hone the command for the future. And the birds were carrying out his orders perfectly.

Emily ran, circling the fire, and joined the Misfits.

Kalagan groaned and flailed as Theo's birds continued to attack. Finally, he grabbed his cape and spiraled his arm, swirling the fabric to create a barrier

between himself and the doves. They scattered up toward the rooftops. A moment later, the cape fell in a heap to the ground.

The man had vanished again.

Fear must have been keeping Theo upright, because now his knees buckled and he collapsed to the asphalt. Emily caught his shoulders before his head could hit the ground. Carter and Leila and Ridley and the twins circled him. He stared up at them, and then past them at the stars, where once he had dreamed that he could fly. His neck stung where the wand had scraped him, but when he held his hand there, his palm came away dry. Thankfully.

Worried voices overlapped. "Is he okay?"

"Did he faint?"

"We should go get help."

"Let's carry him out of here."

Someone called to them from nearby. "Children!"

A figure in a dark cape and a top hat emerged from the alleyway.

Kalagan was back! Theo tried to sit up, but his body refused to move.

Leila leapt to her feet. "Dad!" she called out, and dashed toward him. This was when Theo noticed the white hair peeking out from under the brim of the hat. Leila threw her arms around Mr. Vernon and squeezed him with all her might. "You're all right," she said over and over, until finally he held her away and glanced to the others.

"Yes, I am." He kissed Leila's forehead. Then, meeting Theo's eyes, he asked, "But are *you*?"

Emily used her shoulder to help prop him up, then bring him to his feet. Ridley came to his other side so that he could hold on to her armrest. Her face was drained of color, and her eyes were wet. "I think so," Theo answered woozily.

"Mr. Vernon!" Carter exclaimed, running over to their mentor. "The magic shop is gone!"

Mr. Vernon's face was grave. "I know. My train arrived shortly before it happened. Thank goodness the Other Mr. Vernon is up at the resort. But that's not important right now. Come along," he said, waving for them to follow him into the alley. "We need to get all of you checked out. There is a swarm of ambulances by the park...."

Theo stopped listening as they headed back toward the town green. He could not help but think that the man who had hurt him was still watching from somewhere in the darkness.

He glanced back once more and saw the burning figure crumble to the ground, spraying embers up into the air.

TWENTY-FIVE

For Theo Stein-Meyer, the next few memories passed like a fog through his mind.

Sometimes, however, there were moments of clarity.

He would recall spending several days in the Mineral Wells medical clinic, where the doctors kept him for observation. They said he was suffering from shock, which Theo thought sounded more like a reaction to a very interesting magic trick than a serious medical condition. His parents alternated sitting at his bedside. In the meantime, he had plenty of visitors: his brothers and sisters, the two Mr. Vernons, and of course the other members of the Magic Misfits.

Everyone helped him catch up on what was happening out in the world.

The Vernons' shop had been destroyed. Carter and Leila and both Mr. Vernons had taken a suite at the Grand Oak Resort. Top Hat, Presto, and Change-O were safe there.

While exploring the bootlegging tunnels below the town, investigators had discovered evidence that someone had indeed set off an explosive underneath the magic shop.

The *Mineral Wells Gazette* had printed an article about the radio transmitters inside the Darling Daniels. Now, instead of finding the dolls in all corners of the town, one was most likely to discover a doll peeking out from the top of a garbage can sitting at the end of a driveway or parked in an alley.

Much like Vernon's Magic Shop, Meridian's Music had closed its doors, but for a very different reason. Leila and Carter had gone to check on Emily and Mick and had discovered a note taped to the front window. It read: *To our beloved customers—The time has come for the*

Meridians to move along. Thank you for your many years of patronage. We wish you the best in your future musical endeavors. Fondly, Mick and Emily Meridian.

Theo would not allow himself to believe that she was gone, not without seeing the proof for himself. On the morning he was discharged from the clinic, he asked his parents to drive past the music shop.

The windows were dark. When he got out of the car and pressed his face to the glass, he saw that the instruments that had lined the walls were gone. All that was left were the wires and hooks that had held them aloft for so long.

Returning to the car at the curb, Theo felt an emptiness growing inside him. Where once he had felt his heart beating strongly, there was only a hollow echoing.

★ ★ ★

Almost a week later, Theo joined his friends at the Grand Oak Resort for a private brunch. The Other Mr. Vernon had prepared eggs Florentine, piles of blueberry pancakes, lemon-poppy scones, and enormous donuts of all flavors and colors.

They were the only group in the dining room—the tall, broad doors were shut against the resort's other guests.

Ridley drummed her fingers on the table, gathering their attention. "After thinking about the anagram that Kalagan put on the poster," she said, opening her notebook, "I did some playing around with Darling Daniel's messages. There were six of them, remember?" She turned the notebook around for everyone to see:

Made of wood but filled with laughs!

You will not believe your eyes and ears.

Look no farther than the Grand Oak Resort.

No time like now to get your tickets.

Escape your boring lives with Darling Daniel!

Now you see me!

"We remember," Theo answered. "But what are we supposed to be looking at?"

Leila squeaked. "Oh no!" She looked to her father. "Dad, this is scary!"

Dante Vernon was at the head of the table, wearing a grim expression.

"Will someone please share the secret?" Carter pleaded. Leila dragged her finger down the side of the page, touching the first word of each sentence. Carter read them aloud: "*Made. You. Look. No. Escape...*" He turned the color of the bone china laid out on the table. "*Now,*" he finished with a gulp.

Theo felt his scalp tingle. The twins simply stared at the notebook in horror.

"Kalagan is still nowhere to be found," said Mr. Vernon. "And Ridley's discovery does not bode well for the Magic Misfits or their future."

"What do you mean?" Theo asked. "I thought we were better than ever."

"And that's the problem," said Mr. Vernon. "Kalagan must not believe that."

"You mean..." Carter started, looking puzzled. "What do you mean?"

Ridley crossed her arms. "He means that Mick and Emily had the right idea." She stared at the older magician as if trying to read his mind. "He thinks we shouldn't meet anymore."

"Really, Dad?" Leila asked, glancing around the table. "But we have to. These are my friends. My *best* friends. And they always will be."

Vernon cleared his throat. "Ridley is right. I think the time has come for the Magic Misfits to disband."

Theo felt a creeping sensation across his skin.

Olly sat up straight. "I'll be better," he said. "No more distractions. Only magic."

"Me too," said Izzy. "I've always hated distractions anyway. Distractions are *soooo* distracting. We'll help everyone keep practicing!"

Vernon shook his head. "As long as Kalagan believes that you all are working against him, that you are my own little helpers, he will not stop coming. For you. For *us*. I don't mean to frighten you, but...I am worried. Appearing together as you have been this summer will only be more and more dangerous. Kalagan *must not see* that anymore."

Something about the way Vernon said that last bit lodged in Theo's mind.

Must not see...

"But Mr. Vernon," Carter went on, "we've already agreed. If Kalagan were still here in Mineral Wells, we would know it. Even if he was wearing a disguise, he couldn't hide what happened to his knee when Emily kicked him. We heard the pop. All we need to do is keep a lookout for someone with an injury."

"I'm afraid that will not be enough," said Mr. Vernon. "After what I learned on my recent journey north, I fear that he has ways to circumvent suspicion."

Leila scowled. "You're still not going to tell us what happened while you were away?"

Her father blinked. "I can only apologize for not being here for you all. After Sandra Santos showed up last month, I should have told you that Mick Meridian was a member of the Emerald Ring. Living right here in Mineral Wells. I suppose I need to learn to accept that secrets, while important in magic, hurt more often than they help when real life is concerned."

"So, what do we do now?" Ridley asked. "Just stop talking to each other?"

Vernon looked down. "Keep up the charade. Pretend that you have grown apart. That you cannot get along any longer. Only then will the target be removed from your backs. I am so sorry that I have put us in this situation."

The Misfits glanced around the table at one another. They had no words. There was nothing more to say.

★ ★ ★

The first few days without his friends were the hardest. Theo had his brothers and sisters to keep him company, but their long visit was coming to an end.

"Until next year," said Leo, hugging Theo good-bye from the front porch of their family's house. "Keep up with that violin. It will do you good."

August drew to a close. Theo prepared for the upcoming school year. His parents bought him a new tuxedo to replace the one he had dirtied over the summer. He hurried to read the several books that his English teacher had assigned.

One afternoon, he discovered a letter in the mailbox with his name on it. There was no stamp, no postmark, no return address. Inside was a neatly folded letter. And tucked inside the letter was a mysterious brass key. It fell out into the palm of his hand as he read:

> *Dear Theo,*
>
> *I'm so sorry I never had the chance to say good-bye. Despite everything that happened this summer, I want you to know that I enjoyed the time I spent with you. My father was afraid that if we stayed in Mineral Wells, our shop would have been targeted just like Vernon's Magic Shop.*
>
> *I'm writing to you in confidence that my family*

*feels safer where we are now. My mother and father
are trying to work things out. I know it's not going to
be easy, and that it'll take time. Love is as complicated
as the insides of a metronome. But then, time is
something that we have a lot of now. And I hope that
in time I can give you a real good-bye.*

And maybe someday, another hello.

Yours truly,
Emily Meridian

Wiping away tears, Theo tucked the letter in the drawer next to his bed. He grasped the key in his fist. Then he headed out toward Main Street, walking slowly so he would not bring attention to himself.

He listened to the sounds of every car that passed, to every child shouting from a backyard swing set; he listened for phantom footfalls that might, at any moment, come racing up behind him. He wished that Ridley could accompany him, but he knew that appearing with her would be even more dangerous than walking through Mineral Wells alone.

Theo paused as he came to the corner where Vernon's Magic Shop had stood a few weeks prior. Now

there was only an empty lot. Even the basement had been filled in. It looked like someone had taken a giant eraser and rubbed one of the most iconic parts of Mineral Wells off the map. He continued on, breathing heavily as he approached his destination.

The windows of the old music store were still dark, and they reflected Theo's own solemn face back at him. He took the brass key from his pocket and slid it into the front door. Just as he had expected, the bolt turned easily.

But why had Emily sent him the key?

Theo made his way to the back of the shop, feeling the loneliness of the empty shelves where countless instruments once lived, the abandoned workbench where Mick built his whimsical gadgets. On the workbench itself, though, sat a small parcel. Holding his breath, Theo grabbed the object and brought it back out into the light at the front of the store.

The package was rectangular in shape and smaller than a bread box. It had been wrapped in brown butcher paper and tied neatly with twine. A note was attached. It read: *Keep safe*. He glanced around the shop, making sure that this was not a trap, that no one was hiding, waiting to step out from the shadows, a knife glinting in their fist. He slipped outside and turned the key, locking the shop once again.

A few steps from the door, Theo's curiosity got the best of him. He pulled the twine, then tore off the butcher paper.

It was a wooden box intricately inlaid with multi-colored pieces. It did not appear to have a lid, nor any other obvious way to open it. After a moment, Theo realized that the inlay spelled out letters.

MXM.

It took Theo several seconds to realize why the box looked familiar. When Carter had arrived in Mineral Wells in the spring, he had brought one almost exactly like it with him. The letters on his box were *LWL*. And Leila had discovered another one in the basement of the lodge of the Grand Oak Resort. That one had been marked *AIS*.

Theo knew that the letters were initials. The *AIS* box had belonged to Sandra Santos, the psychic, whose first name was really Alessandra. *LWL* was Lyle Locke, Carter's father. Which meant that *MXM* was Mick Meridian.

Keep safe, the note read. The words made Theo remember what Kalagan had said to him and Carter and Leila outside the ruined magic shop.

Not safe.

Theo shivered and tucked the box inside his jacket. He wished he could ask the Misfits what they thought about this. Why would Mick have left this box behind for Theo? Was there something hidden inside?

At home, Theo made room for the *MXM* box at the back of his closet, on the shelf behind his extra bed pillows. He was not sure if it was the *safest* spot, but it would have to do for now. Or at least until he could get more information.

He took his violin downstairs, made his way out into the backyard, and approached the coop where his doves perched, cooing. Peeking inside, he noticed three small rolls of paper lying on the floor. He swung the chicken-wire door wide and scooped them up.

Making his way into the yard, Theo sat down in the chair where Leo had practiced his cello earlier in the summer, then opened each scroll. He took a special coin out of his pocket so that he could decipher the writing inside. Then he opened his violin case, removed a small pad of paper, and tore a page into three pieces. He checked the coin, wrote out his own message three times, then rolled up each piece and went back to the coop.

After attaching one scroll each to the legs of three

birds, he set the doves free, watching as they flew toward the setting sun. One was headed for Ridley's house, while the two others flapped toward the resort—to the twins and to Carter and Leila.

Theo did not worry. He knew they would come back soon.

He returned to his open violin case and pulled his magic bow from his pocket. He held it aloft, and moments later, the violin rose up to meet his hand like an old friend. He placed it under his chin and raised the bow to the strings.

Music floated and swirled on the wind, dancing and looping in the air around the Stein-Meyer home, and farther up into the sky over Mineral Wells.

As he moved the bow rapidly, then languidly, then with staccato bursts, Theo allowed his emotions to swell. He felt happiness and loneliness and pride all at the same time. He didn't know what would come next, but he wasn't about to stop now. The rhythm danced and swayed, but it always kept time, just like the metronome that sat on the desk in his bedroom.

Tick, tock, tick, tock, tick, tock...

HOW TO...

Make a Card Rise Up from a Deck

If you have been paying attention, you may remember that during the first magic lesson in this book, I asked you to mark the page so you could find it again. For those of you clever enough to have done so, go back and find that first magical moment. (Look for your bookmark. Or feather, or rose petal, or fake mustache!) For those of you clever enough to realize that I would remind you about all this later on, go back and look on page 24. Do not worry. You are not cheating.

Did you find the trick? It is the one called "How to Find a Spectator's Card."

Splendid! You can use the *following* trick as a continuation of that first trick, or you may simply do this trick on its own. Either way should delight your audience and make them want to pat your back.

WHAT YOU'LL NEED:

A regular deck of playing cards

STEPS:

1. Go ahead and try that first trick with a volunteer.

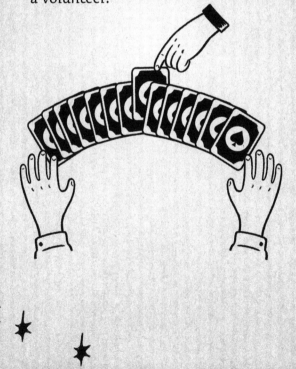

2. Once you have located the volunteer's card, cut the deck in two. When you reunite the two piles, make sure that their card is on the top of the stack.

3. In one hand, hold the deck with the suits facing your audience so that they see the bottom card. The card on the top of the deck will be the one that your volunteer chose.

THEIR CARD!

4. With your other hand, hold your pointer finger just over the top of the deck, so that your finger points away from you.

5. Explain that the tip of your finger is filled with so much magic it can make a card rise out of the deck. You might try blowing on your finger beforehand, or even rubbing it on your shirt, as if "charging" it.

6. Slowly lower your hand so that your finger rests on top of the deck.

SECRET MAGIC MOVE:

As you bring your pointer finger down, extend your pinky finger of the same hand so that it is touching the back of the deck. Keep this move hidden from your audience.

7. Slowly raise your pointer finger while pressing the tip of your pinky against the top card. Use your pinky to move the card upward. Astound your audience as the volunteer's card appears to rise shockingly out of the deck, as if attached to your "magically charged" pointer finger.

8. To maintain the illusion, when the card is about halfway up, use your pointer finger and thumb to grab the top of the card and pull it away from the rest, while quickly tucking your pinky finger into your palm. Hand the card to the volunteer.

9. Smile and take a well-deserved bow.

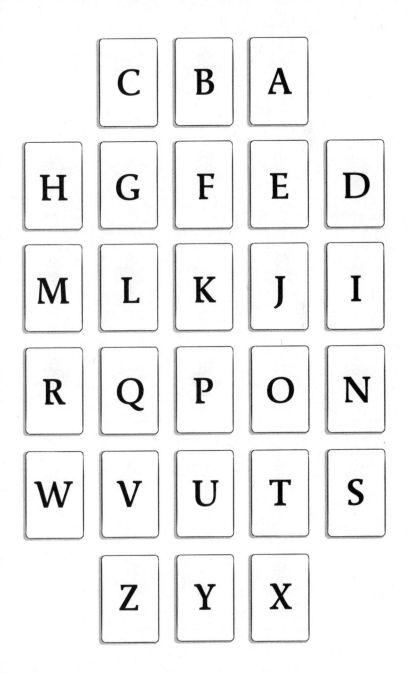

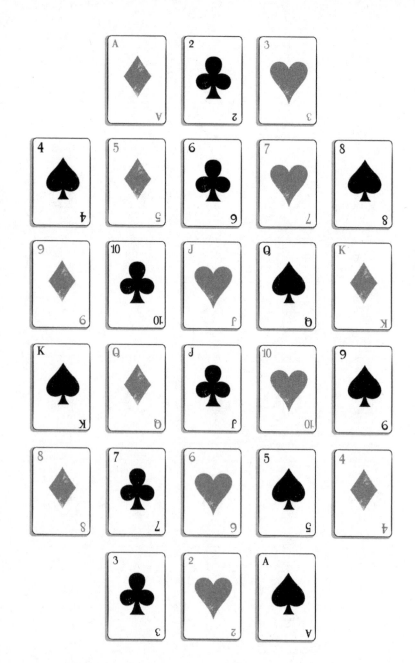

FAREWELL, FOR NOW

Thank you, dear reader, for choosing to spend your time with me, and with the Magic Misfits. I know the end of this tale must feel rather heart-wrenching, but do not despair. There is another story to come.

What a tale it will be!

Adventure, laughs, deception, revelation, and more magic than can be safely experienced in one sitting. Like the twine wrapped around the package in Meridian's Music, I promise that all your questions will be answered, tied up in a bow.

I cannot say that the bow will be pretty.

Nevertheless, a bow it will be.

You might be wondering what was written in the scrolls that Theo discovered inside the bird coop. I have included the transcripts. You may read them if you can decode them, just like Theo had to do.

When you are finished, make sure you take the time to hug your loved ones. Thank your friends for being your friends. Your family for being your family. Go out and create some wonder. Make some magic. At this point, you should have plenty in supply. Your loved ones will be filled with gratitude for your bringing smiles to their faces, as I am filled with gratitude for you, my friend.

Until next time: Be brilliant, be brave, be curious, be kind. Be a misfit.

Be the magic you wish to make in this world.

THE DOVE CODES

Jfrvg sviv. Nrhh blf zoo.— O & X

Nliv wlooh zg gsv ivhlig. Glhhvw gsvn lfg orpv
bvhgviwzb'h mvdh.— L & R

Dliprmt lm hlnvgsrmt yrt. Nliv gl xlnv.— I

Ulfmw hlnvgsrmt. Nvvg zg gsv hvxivg olxzgrlm
glnliild?—♥ G

— ACKNOWLEDGMENTS —

Special thanks to the following carnies who ran away to join my circus: Deirdre "the Ringmaster" Jones, Laura "the Lion Tamer" Nolan, Zoë "the Mentalist" Chapin, Dan "the Ventriloquist" Poblocki, Lissy "the Tattooed Woman" Marlin and Kyle "the Tattooed Man" Hilton, Jonathan "the Prestidigitator" Bayme, Timothy "the Magician's Assistant" Meola, David "the Bull Handler" Burtka, and all the Gandy Dancers at Little, Brown, especially Megan Tingley, Karina Granda, and Alvina Ling.

Also, thanks to everyone at the world-famous Magic Castle, home to the Academy of Magical Arts. It's the greatest clubhouse in existence for grown-up misfits like me, and continues to inspire countless people to pick up a wand and learn some new skills. I doff my top hat to you all.

— ABOUT THE AUTHOR —

Neil Patrick Harris is still an accomplished actor, producer, director, host, author, husband, magician, and father of effulgent twins. Harris also served as president of the Academy of Magical Arts from 2011 to 2014, so there. The *New York Times* bestselling Magic Misfits series was his middle-grade debut.

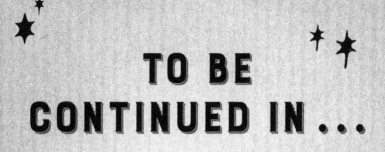

TO BE
CONTINUED IN ...